The Enemy

Kings Of Ruin: Book 5

L Knight

The Enemy
Kings of Ruin Book Five
By L Knight

Published by L Knight
Cover: Clem Parsons-Metatec
Editing: Black Opal Editing
Formatting: Black Opal Editing

Prologue: Hudson

10 years ago.

"You make me feel normal."

I lift my head my gaze to find Audrey, her mesmerizing eyes that sometimes look moss green and sometimes a twinkling hazel depending on her mood, looking at me. My lips pull at the edges, and I find myself wanting to smile, my chest full, a tingle where my heart beats. I haven't had a life with a lot to smile about but this girl makes all of it fade away. I roll my body, pinning her supple softness to the bed where we just made love, my body looming over her, and I realize that I'd cut my chest open and bleed on the ground at her feet if she asked me to. It's terrifying how much I feel for her, how much she owns me. Only one other person has that from me, and she's the woman who gave me life. I stroke my fingers gently down her soft cheek and consider her words. I never want to make Audrey feel normal, I want her to feel special and adored every single day.

"I'm sorry, Belle."

Her lips twitch at the name I have taken to calling her when we're alone. My Belle, all that beauty both inside and out, but that's not why I call her Belle. It's because, to me, she's like that Disney character, smart and willing to challenge the world around her, rather than do what is expected. She is fierce and I love that about her. Her head tilts to the side and she gives me a quizzical look.

"Why are you sorry?"

Genuine confusion creases her forehead and I try to smooth it away with a swipe of my thumb, my hand caressing her cheek before my thumb tugs on her bottom lip as I gaze at her. She's so fucking sexy, and I can feel my cock lengthen as I lie cradled between her thighs. The silky wet feel of her pussy makes me groan as I rock my hips gently, the crown of my cock nudging against her sensitive clit. Her body shudders and I want to drink down the whimper that escapes from her throat. To own every single noise past her lips, as if it's mine because I want everything she is to be mine because everything of me is hers. She sees me, she sees past the cheap clothes, and the death trap of a bike I ride. She sees the man I want to be, the man I will be, not the boy who has no right attending ts prestigious college filled with rich kids. Who is so broke that some days Ramen is a luxury; who, without his scholarship, would never be able to attend the school that is educating the future politicians and business icons of the world.

"I never want you to feel normal, Aud, not when you're the most precious, amazing, smart, beautiful person to ever walk this planet." I lower my head, my lips brushing hers, trying to imbue everything I feel for her into my kiss. Her head tilts and she sighs and I drink it down as her tongue swipes against mine. The heat simmers but it's the emotion passing between us that leaves me breathless as I break away to stare at her.

"You should feel extraordinary because you're all those things. You floor me with wonder every time you smile at me. That I could be the lucky bastard who gets to be with you, when I don't deserve to breathe the same air as you, truly astounds me."

Tears gild her eyes in silver and my heart seizes. I hate seeing her tears. They slay me and make me want to fight wars for her, just to stop a single one from falling. I love this woman, with my whole heart, and I know we haven't said it in so many words, but I hope what I just said somehow feels even more special than a simple 'I love you'.

I've only ever said those words to my mother, the woman who raised me alone, who has suffered more in her life than I can ever imagine. She is why I strive to be better, she's the person who made me who I am, and I never forget that, but Audrey is my hope, my joy, and one day my wife, if I'm a lucky enough bastard.

I dip my head and skim my lips over hers, swiping my tongue over the plump flesh and she sighs as her legs twine around my hips, seeking more. I rest my weight on either side of her head on my forearms, caging her in, and position my cock at her entrance. No words are necessary as our eyes meet, our souls dancing as I slowly thrust into her tight, wet heat.

Her head moves back, arching her neck to me as she moans, her body clenching around my dick as I begin to fuck her slowly. Long, slow thrusts that connect us in every way. My lips pepper her with open-mouthed kisses along her delicate throat as she fists her hands through my hair, her fingernails scraping my scalp. I feel it right the way to my cock, my body trembling with need to come.

"Hudson..."

Her voice is smoky and breathless, a silent caress down my senses. Her legs tighten around me as our movements become wild, and restless, as if we're barreling toward something we both know will change everything. Nothing has ever felt like this, a pure white-hot pleasure. I shift slightly, lifting up, so I can lift her thigh beneath her knee and pound into her harder, deeper. I want to consume her, and her body begins to shake.

"Are you close?" I'm fighting my climax, my whole body shaking with the need to come, but not before her.

"Yes...I...."

Then her entire body tightens, her pussy milking my dick, rippling and squeezing, her nails tearing down my back as she falls apart. It is the most beautiful thing I have ever seen. Her heavy-lidded eyes fall open and she looks at me as if I am the answer to every question the universe has ever asked.

"I love you."

My climax hits me at the same time her words do, and I feel like I'm having an out-of-body experience as my orgasm pumps through me, spurts of my hot come filling her as I bellow like a king.

With my cock twitching the last jets of my release into her, I sag against her body. I feel drained, turned inside out. I love this woman and I know that tonight just changed everything. For the first time in a long time, I have hope.

Long fingers sift through my hair as I hold her to me, my head resting against her lush breasts, which I didn't give nearly enough attention to this last time. I pull a tight nipple between my lips, tugging and nipping as her pussy flexes around my softening cock. I let her go with a pop and drop a light kiss on her belly, as I roll off her.

"You, okay?"

I turn my head to look at her and smile, a true happy-to-the-bones-of-my-soul grin. I still have a lot to tell her about my family, and my circumstances but I feel like we have time. I can take her to meet my mom, who'll love her and, maybe, just maybe, one day I can be good enough for her, although I somehow doubt that.

"I'm better than fine. You make me happy, Audrey, really happy." I don't say I love you back, because I don't want her to think I'm saying it because she did. I want to do something special for her.

"I never knew how happy I could be until I met you, Hudson Carmichael."

She smiles and turns, swinging her legs over the side of the bed. "I need to get showered before we meet the others. I don't want to meet my cousin smelling of sex."

I don't know her friends well, but they seem like decent people, and Lincoln is her cousin and they're close. "Want some company?"

She flashes me a sexy smirk. "No way, buster. If you come in here, we won't get out of here tonight."

"I don't see the problem." I'm joking but I'd be more than happy to stay here and hold her in my arms rather than socialize with people who make the differences between us look so huge that we're barely the same species.

"I know but I want you to get to know them. They're important to me, and so are you."

"Fine, go shower. I'll keep myself occupied." I kick the sheet down and fist my already hardening cock, stroking and fisting it as her eyes go hooded. Fuck, this girl is sin on a stick.

Her tongue slips out to wet her lips and I groan and release my cock. "Later, I want those lips around my cock."

"Yes."

Before I can tackle her to the bed, she slams the bathroom door with a giggle, the lock clicking loudly in the room. I smile wide at how shy she can sometimes be, insisting on locking the bathroom door when she uses the toilet, when I've had my mouth on every inch of her perfect body. She's complex and so far out of my league, and yet she said she loves me, and I feel like a king because of it. I try to think of anything but her in an effort to get my dick to go down but, surrounded by her scent and the smell of sex, it's impossible. I stand and grab my jeans to check my phone and curse when I see a flurry of missed calls from my mom.

I try to call her back and get nothing but there is a text waiting.

Mom: It's happening. Can you meet me there?

Fuck!

I shove my clothes on, listening to the sound of the shower, and know I should tell Audrey what's going on, but I need to go. I can't leave my mom alone when she needs me. I look around desperately and find a scrap of torn paper. I can leave her a note and explain. I root around the room for a pen and find one covered in flowers with a fluffy pink pom-pom on the end. My lips twitch at the sight even with panic unfurling in my belly. I quickly scribble an explanation that I need to go and will call her later and then prop it against the lamp on her bedside table, cursing when the flimsy paper keeps falling. I prop it again so she'll see it and it finally stays. I sigh in relief and cast one more glance at the bathroom door, wishing I could explain in person, but Audrey knows nothing of my life, of my background. Something I regret fiercely right now, but I'll explain everything. The sound of her singing eases the giant knot in my gut. My mom will love Audrey almost as much as I do. And with that sense of excitement and nerves in my belly, I leave, clicking the door shut and racing for my bike, the note I left her fluttering off the nightstand with the light puff of air from the door closing and landing in the wastepaper basket.

1. Audrey

Looking at Eden, it's easy to see the utter radiant joy on her face as she moves down the aisle as if walking on air, towards Ryker. It blooms and spills from her as if it can't be contained and I guess a part of that is because she's four months pregnant. I tilt my head toward my friend who stands tall and handsome at the head of the alter with our other friends, Harrison, Beck, and my cousin Lincoln as his groomsmen beside him.

The way he looks at his bride almost steals my breath from my lungs. Such unabashed adoration that he makes no effort to conceal as the tears fall fat and freely down his sharp cheekbones. Love: that rare, and precious emotion fills the room, and it is all I can do not to flee, not to run screaming as regret and pain lances through me like the dull blade of a rusty dagger. Not when the man who stole that sweet promise of unadulterated love and a future filled with hope away from me stands not fifteen feet away.

A ball of hate worms in my gut, like snakes twining around each other, hissing and spitting their displeasure. Hudson Carmichael, who took the love of a naive young woman desperate to be seen, and stamped it into the ground with his callous boot. I feel his hot, dark gaze on me, tendrils of seductive heat skating down my skin and fight the urge to give in and look at him. Why does he still have the ability to make me crave him and at the same time hate him beyond all measure of sense?

My control was a hard-won battle and only years of being this Audrey, this cool, unemotional woman who doesn't feel, allows me to keep my eyes pinned on the bride and groom as they make their vows to each other with such unabashed adoration skating through every word that my breath hitches and my hands shake.

I've watched from the sidelines as each one of my friends has found the one, or two in Beck's case, who makes them whole, who makes them complete in a way they could never be on their own. I've cheered for every single one of them with genuine heartfelt joy when they found what they were looking for, but the hollow ache in my chest grows each day. Like a cancer eating away at a bit more of me until I'm unsure if there'll be anything left to bury when I finally leave this world.

I find myself turning towards the pull he has on me, caving to the urge for just a second and lock eyes with Hudson Carmichael. His eyes are the palest blue, almost silvery, and they pin me in place, his expression intense and unreadable. His jaw is sharp and strong with just the slightest scruff on it. A proud chin, which he holds high, giving him the look of an arrogant fallen angel.

My fingers tingle, remembering the silky thickness of his hair sliding against my skin. He wears it shorter now than the unruly waves which I loved, but he looks no less devastating, and I hate that, with each year I age, he seems to grow more devastatingly handsome. Hudson could have been on the cover of Vogue, he looked so edible in that damn tux, but then he wears a leather jacket and distressed jeans just as well. Like a chameleon. No, not a chameleon, something more because Hudson doesn't blend into his surroundings, he owns them like a Greek god sent to walk among the mortals.

The Enemy

I school my expression into one of unforgiving hate and boredom as I let my gaze slide over him. I want him to feel as worthless as he made me feel all those years ago. Yet, when I look up, he has the sexiest smirk on his full lips, a slight quirk of his left eyebrow, a challenge, like he can read my thoughts and see straight through them to the damaged decaying heart that still only beats for him. As if he knows a secret that he has no intention of sharing. It makes me indescribably angry and, for one second, I feel my body lean as if I'll march over there and what? What will I do? Nothing because it's hard to know what to do when you despise the person you love the most. When his downfall is my greatest desire and yet knowing that, by destroying him, I'll burn down the last shred of myself until there's nothing but cold black ash to prove I ever lived.

My body is hot, aching, desperate for his touch, but my mind wants to shred him into tiny bits. I snap back to reality, my gaze breaking away from his and straighten my shoulders, lifting my chin in defiance as I hear the whoops and whistles and see Ryker bending Eden over backward and kissing her like she's the air he needs to live. That brings a small smile to my face, and I thrust any thoughts of Hudson from my brain. He doesn't deserve any headroom and I won't give it to him, not today. This is a happy day, and I won't allow him to poison it. I won't allow him to take one more thing from me.

I stay focused on Ryker and Eden as they head back up the aisle and Lincoln meets me to escort me on the short walk to the church doors. I hold onto his arm like a lifeline, composing myself for the afternoon ahead. My cousin is the only person in the world who knows some of what transpired between Hudson and I, and as if sensing my earlier discomfort, he dips his head to check on me.

"Are you okay, cous? You look like you want to maim someone."

It's funny, I've worked so hard to hide my pain from everyone, to hide how broken I am that every person I love believes the lie I've sold them. That I'm this strong, smart, force of nature who isn't to be crossed. In some ways that is true, I am that person, and I don't regret

3

that. I like who I am, who I fought to become to survive. I love my friends and I'm fiercely loyal to those I let into my small circle, but sometimes I wish I could drop my guard for just a little while and be the girl who once saw the joy in everything.

I slide my gaze to Hudson as we walk past, giving him a withering look and Lincoln snickers.

"Want me to punch him for you, Aud?"

"We are not five, Lincoln."

"No, but it would be fun."

I smile and shake my head. I love my cousin, faults and all because, no matter what, he's loyal, and he stepped up for me. I'll never forget that. "No, he isn't worth the trouble it will cause you with Lottie."

Lincoln looks like he swallowed a wasp. "I still can't believe she likes that asshole. Of all the people for my wife to have a bleeding heart for, it's him."

"He helped her when she needed it." I don't know why I say it. Defending Hudson is never something I want to do, but it's the truth. He went to bat for my cousin's wife, and in some ways my cousin too, when he helped put my uncle away for his vicious crimes against Lottie's mother, amongst others. My dislike of Hudson will never stop me from being honest about that. Being honest with myself is something I pride myself on, which is why I can admit if only to myself that no matter what, I'll always love the man I hate so much. Whatever he did to me, and my gut clenches with the whisper of pain at the thought, he was good to my friends.

"Yeah, he was, and that's the only reason he's still standing."

We make it out of the little chapel in Vegas where Ryker and Eden wanted their wedding, and the sun beats down on us, hot and relentless. My skin warms where it's exposed by the strapless, champagne-colored sheath dress all of the bridesmaids are wearing. Lottie was asked to be a bridesmaid but declined after admitting she was pregnant and barely keeping any food down. She wanted to be able to run from the room if she needed without causing a commotion. She insisted Lincoln remain as a groomsman though, hence him leading me out, although he hadn't been happy about being more than two feet from her. Lincoln was taking overprotective to another level. If he had his way, Lottie would be on bed rest and not lift a finger until the day she gave birth and if he could arrange her birth plan, he would. Lucky for us and him, Lottie has grown a lot in the time they've been together and knows exactly how to manage her husband and when to put her foot down and this was one of those times.

"So it's not because messing with him would mean a week on the couch if Lottie found out?"

"Yeah, that too. I love my wife, and since we got back together, she has this iron will that I find oddly arousing, but the threat to my manhood, not so much."

"Is it wrong that I love how much she owns your ass?"

Lincoln gets this soft look as his head lifts and he searches her out, his eyes full of love when he finds her. "How could it be wrong when I love it too?"

"I'm happy for you, Lincoln."

"I almost lost her with my stupidity and deplorable behavior, but she gave me another chance. I won't waste it."

"I know."

"Audrey, can I escort you to the venue?"

I release Lincoln as I turn to my date, trying to force a smile to my lips and hide the irritation his mere breathing makes me feel. My smile is pinched, and the sound of his voice annoys me to no end, but he serves a purpose, namely to keep Hudson away from me. Joe, Jerry, Jed, I can't remember his name, is classically handsome with blond hair and blue eyes and a body that shows the hours he spends in the gym. I wish he was as good in bed as his body and looks promised, but unfortunately, Jed, John, Jonah, whatever his name is, couldn't find the clit with a fucking SatNav.

Jason, that's it! I focus on him as he offers his arm in a gallant move, he probably thinks is suave and sexy, but only makes me cringe. I'm about to reject him when I glance up and see Hudson watching us with a dark, brooding look on his face. God, he's a handsome bastard. I let my eyes wander over him, not toning down my obvious pursual, and find myself clenching my thighs together. I want to make him feel small, like an object with no value to me. I lift my head back to him and our eyes meet. He smirks and it's like he can read my mind and I want to slap that smug look off his face. I give him the cool, haughty look of someone superior to him and turn to Jason with a wide smile.

"Of course, you can escort me, you handsome boy."

He seems to have no idea I just insulted him to his face, calling him a boy when he's surrounded by men. Jason is nothing but a toy to me, and it's just how I like it. I don't allow men to get close to me. I treat them like dirt under my shoes and they let me because of my wealth, my name, and because the chance to screw me delights them. They all think they can tame me, can manipulate me into falling in love with them, when in truth, it will never happen. Men believe I'm a plaything, but I'm the hunter, and they're the prey. I was prey once before and it will never happen again.

Jason's bright white teeth almost blind me as he walks me to the hotel that is owned by our friend Ethan Masters. He also owns the Manhattan Cleavers hockey team. His family and mine have been friends for years, both old money that goes back generations. When Ethan found out about Ryker getting married, he offered the hotel as a venue as his wedding gift to the happy couple. He's a few years older than me, and his sister Serenity is an actress who just got a part on a new streaming show that promises to be the hit of the year.

Jason is still prattling on about stocks and share prices when we step into the room where the reception will be held but I've tuned him out. It is truly beautiful inside the high-ceilinged room. All pale pinks and rose gold with cream flowers and just that touch of sparkle that defines Eden and Ryker together. I feel incredibly honored that Eden allowed me to help her with it, and that we've become close. My friends, the boys I met in college who have been my family, have been incredibly lucky with the women they've found, and so have I. I consider each one of them part of my family and they've given me something I never had before. A sisterhood, a group of women who have my back in ways my male friends can't. I love those boys like brothers, but Norrie, Lottie, Amelia, and Eden have become the sisters I always wanted.

So why don't you tell any of them the truth about who you really are?

Because I'll lose them, they'll pity me, and I can't stand the thought.

I suffer through the three-course meal, barely tasting any of the beautiful food that Eden took ages choosing. I chat with Norrie and Harrison, ignoring the questioning looks my friend gives me. We're seated at a round table of ten. Me and Jason, Norrie and Harrison, Lincoln and Lottie, Eric, and Beck, Xander, and Amelia. We have a shorthand that friendships, as long and as deep as ours, have, and the conversation ebbs and flows naturally. Jason is trying to engage Lincoln in some business scheme, and I should feel bad as I watch my date being played with like a spider with a fly in his web, but he brought it on himself. I warned him no business at the wedding, and he chose not to listen. If Lincoln eviscerates him, it's his own fault.

Jason turns to me when Lincoln gets bored and shuts him down, turning his attention to his wife.

"Champagne?"

I have a slight tension headache from resisting the urge to seek out Hudson, but I nod regardless, hoping the alcohol will ease the strain in my neck. "Yes, please."

Jason looks around for a waiter, but I need a few minutes away from him, away from all of this to get my game face on before I face everyone at the table for speeches. I'm like a glass statue, hard and impossible to scratch but one wrong move and I could shatter into a thousand shards and cut everyone around me into ribbons.

"Actually, would you mind getting me an Old Fashioned instead?"

Jason takes my hand and kisses my knuckles, and it takes everything in me not to cringe. This man gives me the ick in a big way, but I smile through gritted teeth, wondering how much my dentist will cry when he sees the damage I'm doing to my molars from grinding them.

"Anything for my girl."

Beck snorts and mumbles something as Amelia nudges him in the ribs.

Urgh.

It's on the tip of my tongue to tear Jason down a peg and remind him exactly who I am, but I have no intention of causing a scene over someone who doesn't matter. Not today. Not when Eden and Ryker deserve every moment of happiness after what they went through to get here.

I watch Jason walk away and almost lose an eyeball I roll my eyes so hard. I stand and excuse myself with a practiced smile before I head toward the doors, my stride sure, my mind elsewhere. I turn sharply near the bar that leads to the exit to find a private moment on the terrace and crash into a hard, immovable object. I reach out and steady myself as a big hand grips my biceps to stop my tumble and that's when I smell his scent. Cedar and lime and fresh sea air. The scent that haunts me and drugs me as much as it repulses me.

My gaze flashes up to his impassive face, and I yank my arm from his grip. "Get your hands off me."

Hudson puts his hands up and takes a step back and it takes all my strength not to step forward and sink into him. To run my hands over his hard chest, to card my fingers through his thick, dark hair and feel the softness, and I hate myself for it.

"Apologies. I merely wished to stop you from falling to the floor at my feet."

I snort, hating how this man can make me lose my composure,

and have me wanting him with a passion that is scalding hot. "You wish, asshole."

His teeth roll his bottom lip and I follow the movement like a drug addict needing a fix.

"You have no idea what I wish, Belle."

"Don't you fucking dare call me that."

"Always so on edge, Miss Kennedy. Are you perhaps a little sexually frustrated?"

Anger clouds my senses. He can unravel me quicker than any other person on the planet.

"Oh, please. I'd rather fuck a cactus than let you touch me."

His eyes travel over my skin, burning a path where they touch. "Hmm, that's not quite true, is it, Audrey? If I remember rightly, you begged me to ruin that sweet pussy with my cock and my mouth."

How dare he bring that up after everything he did. I want to eviscerate him, to wound him and bring him to his knees like he did me. My chest is heaving as I try and fail to contain the temper that is rising in me like a monster ready to eat me whole. "You're the fucking devil, Hudson Carmichael." I scan him from top to bottom, my gaze moving over him before finding his heated stare. I step forward, getting in his face, my lips close to his ear. "The truth is, Hudson, that night when we were oh so young, was an audition and you never got the callback, asshole." I step back, holding my breath so his scent doesn't consume me.

His lips spread into an arrogant grin, and I want to slap it off his face and then tackle him to the floor and take out all my anger on the body I know lies beneath. He dips his head closer, and his scent floods my senses again until I swear I'll never get it out of my nostrils.

"You're a fucking goddess when you're angry, Audrey, and do you want to know a secret?"

I go silent, not trusting myself to speak but unable to move away from him.

"Your pussy is still the sweetest thing I've ever tasted."

"You're a pig."

"Think what you like of me, but it's the truth."

I move in for the kill, needing to end this before I do something I regret. "That's the thing, Hudson. I don't think of you. You're nothing to me, you never were."

Then I turn on my heel and head for the bar, my head held high as I fight not to break down and cry from anger, from vicious memories, and from the fact that he's still the only man who has ever made me feel alive.

2. Hudson

I STAND, WATCHING HER WALK AWAY AND WANT TO PUNCH myself in the face for my inability to stay away from her. I never should've come here. I should've stayed home and caught up on some work or fucking anything but coming here and torturing myself with what I can't have.

Audrey will never be mine, no matter that she haunts my dreams both awake and asleep. I made my choices long ago, and putting us both through this special brand of torture, by hanging around on the periphery of her life just to catch a glimpse, is unfair to us both. So why can't I stop?

I should apologize to her for riling her up, and as my feet guide me to the bar where she sits on a stool, her spine straight her elegant neck long and begging for my touch, that is what I vow to do.

I'm feet from her when the man, who has monopolized her attention all night, cuts across me and slides his arm around her back. I pause, my hand going to my left trouser pocket and flipping the coin through my fingers. Audrey stiffens at his touch and leans away but the stupid prick can't seem to catch a clue as he leans in to try and nuzzle her neck.

It takes everything in me not to slam his face against the bar until he's nothing but a bloody pulp. To tear him apart for touching what is mine, for thinking he's good enough to even breathe the same air as her. He'll never be good enough for her, nobody will. Especially not me, and I know it, but I can't squash the blind jealous rage that slams through me whenever anyone goes near her.

I've tried everything to exorcise the beautiful, frustrating woman from my brain, but she's burrowed so deep, nothing will ever evict her, and I'm not even sure who I'd be without that tiny light that is her that flickers around my heart. She's as much a part of me as my heart, my lungs.

Audrey will always belong to me in some way, even if she doesn't know it, not because I wish to control her or own her, because something as precious as what she makes me feel is not tangible, but because she took my heart so many years ago and never gave it back.

Now, remembering my actions from back then, the empty space in my chest fills with the black tar of guilt. I made my choices, and I don't regret them, at least most of them, but giving up Audrey is the one thing that I wish with all my dead heart I could go back and change.

"Take the fucking hint, Jason. I'm not interested so back up before I drive your balls through your teeth."

Jason chuckles, either not sensing the danger or too stupid to realize she means business.

"Oh, I like it rough. Want to tie me up too, Aud?"

Audrey swivels on her stool to look at him, her neck angled like the queen she is, and I lean my shoulder against a pillar near the entrance to the bar and watch. With any other woman, I'd happily step in, but Audrey would have my head on a stick for interfering and she can handle this, I have no doubt about that. Watching her cock her perfectly arched brow, I almost smile to myself. I've dealt with some of the worst of humanity over the years. Violence is a fact of life. Some people deserve it, most don't, but only the cunning smile of violence on Audrey's face makes my dick hard.

What I wouldn't give to be the man to stand beside her in every battle.

Her hand snaps forward and Jason goes up on tiptoes as she holds his junk. His face pales as she leans forward, and I angle my body to see her expression. She looks like a Valkyrie about to go to war. A woman ready to end empires and she's fucking breath-taking.

"I'm going to say this one time, Jason. Do. Not. Touch. Me without my consent. I'm not going to fuck you, I don't want to see you, hear you, and I sure as hell won't think about you. It wasn't fun, and I won't call. So do yourself a favor and leave before I rip these pathetic balls from your over-muscled body and shove them down your throat."

Fuck.

She releases him and he steps back, his face red now as he tries to regain some of the masculinity that Audrey just put through her verbal mincer. "You were a lousy fuck anyway."

He shoulders past me as she picks up her drink and chuckles. I slide onto the stool beside her and order a whiskey from the bartender, who wisely stayed at the other end until now.

I sip the amber liquid in silence, not really sure how to say I'm sorry when there are so many other things clouding my thoughts. I know I ghosted her. I know I hurt her, and I never believed she'd hate me so intensely for so long, but I also know this apology is well over-due. "I'm sorry."

In my peripheral, I notice her glass pause halfway to her lips before she sips the last of her cocktail and lifts it to the bartender.

"Fuck off, Hudson. I'm not in the mood."

I swing my torso toward her, seeing for the first time the guard she holds so steadily has a chink. She's otherworldly beautiful like a Hollywood starlet had a baby with an angel, and yet today I can see the thing she hides so well. Pain, so deep, so visceral that it carves wounds that aren't healing into her soul.

"I'm not here to make trouble. I just wanted to apologize."

Audrey turns toward me, and I do the same, my legs bracketing her thighs. The gut punch of desire that runs through me every time I'm around her makes me glad I'm sitting down.

"For what?"

"For earlier. For trying to get a rise out of you."

"That it?"

I know now isn't the time or the place for this conversation but, for the first time in years, she's giving me a glimpse of vulnerability, even if she doesn't realize it. "No, but not here. Can we go grab a drink somewhere else and talk? I don't want this animosity between us."

Audrey snorts but it holds no humor, only contempt. "Animosity suits me just fine."

"Are you happy living like this, Belle, with so much hate for a mistake I made years ago?"

Her anger is like a living thing, rising up in her and I want to grab her and kiss her until it consumes us both.

"My life is none of your business."

I notice she doesn't tell me she's happy, and a wave of regret almost takes me under. I don't give a fuck if I'm living half a life without her, but to know she is too almost breaks me. "I know. Just have a drink with me then, for old times' sake. I'll even let you regale me with all the reasons I'm a bastard."

She cocks her head as if I'm a species she doesn't recognize and turns back to the bar, signaling the bartender who hurries over like an eager puppy with a look of adoration on his face. I can't blame him, it's the Audrey effect. She dazzles everyone she meets and has no clue.

"What can I get you?"

The man is probably early twenties and looking at Audrey like she hung the damn moon. I want to offer the guy a fist bump, for having such good taste but then I also want to rip his eyes from their sockets for looking at her like he is with open lust.

Audrey waggles her eyebrows. "Well, isn't that the question of the day, handsome?"

The Enemy

I know she's doing it to rile me, and I won't show her it's working. I won't let Audrey toy with me like I'm a plaything for her enjoyment. It's not in me to be weak. I've fought for everything I have, so being passive and showing weakness isn't my style. Not now, anyway.

Hipster bar kid leans forward with a grin. "I get off at midnight."

"Well, let's hope I'll be getting off too."

She's magnificent. This poor kid doesn't stand a chance of handling her and I'm not sure I do either, but I sure as fuck want to.

"You got it, babe. You want a drink while you wait?"

Pathetic child thinks he can let a woman like Audrey wait for him for hours? He must be smoking some bad shit if that's the case.

"Champagne. He's paying so make it the good stuff."

Audrey looks at me with a challenge and I nod at the kid, who she won't be going home with, to go ahead. "You really think that kid can get you off, Aud?"

"I'm sorry, did I ask for your opinion?"

"Just saying, he probably thinks the G-spot is a band."

Her eyes travel over me with disdain and my dick strains in my pants. "Oh, please. Like you're any better."

"If I remember rightly, Audrey, your actual words were '*Oh, Hudson, fuck me, Hudson, you're the best.*' So based on that, I'm leaps and bounds better."

She sniffs. "I barely remember."

"You never were a good liar."

"Really? I'm an excellent liar."

"Of course, you are. That's why Steve Godsall found out that I was the one who hid basil herbs in his locker just before Principal Jobbie did an inspection."

"I didn't tell him."

Her lips twitch and, for the first time since I walked away from her, I see something other than hate. I want to hold onto it, to wrap it in my arms and cradle the feeling. "Did you know Jobbie is what Scottish people call a shit? Our principal was literally called shit."

Audrey's eyes go wide before she bursts out laughing, her head falling back revealing the slender length of her throat, and it almost steals the breath from my lungs.

"Oh my God, I can't breathe."

We're wheezing our way through our laughter when two glasses of Champagne appear in front of us. Luckily the bartender is now busy as the bar fills up and he leaves us alone.

"I missed this."

Audrey sobers. "Yes, well, we didn't exactly part on good terms, did we?"

"Not bad either. I'm sorry, Audrey."

She puts her hand up to stop me. "No, I can't."

I see it then, the wobble in her composure, and realize I didn't just hurt her, I wrecked her, and I have no right to open old wounds to appease my conscience. "I understand."

I move to stand and give her the peace she deserves but she lays a hand on my forearm. Electricity rips through me at her touch, and I know I'll never have that connection with anyone but her again. I've spent the best part of my adult life searching for anything that felt even half as good and failed. I met the love of my life as a stupid teenager and fucked it up beyond measure. My penance is to live knowing that I'll never have that again. Yet I'm desperate to hold onto this moment, to freeze time and soak up every second of her intense focus aimed at me.

"How about this, we get drunk, have fun, but keep our pants on? No funny stuff. Just old friends spending an evening getting wasted at a biker wedding."

I look around, seeing Eden's family mixing with Ryker's, and smile with a nod. "Deal. But to clarify, that means no sex, right?" Audrey gives me a look that would freeze the balls off most men and I wink. "Just kidding. Friends, fun, and champagne."

"And no feelings of any kind. When tonight is over, we go back to ignoring each other. I can't be your friend again, Hudson."

The quiet way she says it twists inside me, with more impact than if she had screamed at me.

The Enemy

I hate that, but then, what choice do I have?

I roll over in bed and pain lances through my brain like someone took a red-hot poker to my gray cells. My mouth is so dry that my tongue is almost stuck to the roof of my mouth. I roll to sit upright, gently prying my eyes open, and hold my hand up to try and ward off the light coming in through the open drapes of the bedroom. My stomach roils as I swing my feet to the floor and my gaze catches on a naked body.

As I groan and turn to take a closer look, my head an empty expanse of nothing. Shock renders me frozen as I realize it's not just any naked body, but Audrey. My Audrey is naked in bed beside me, and I can't seem to remember a single thing. The sheet is pooled on the curve of her delectable ass, the smooth silky skin of her back making my fingers itch to touch her.

Her dark hair falls over her face in wild disarray as she snores softly, her arms under the pillow allowing me a teasing glimpse of the side of her breasts. Fuck, what did we do? How did we end up here naked in this bed together? I'll be so fucking pissed if we had sex and I was too drunk to remember it, but more than that, I'll be pissed at myself for touching her when she was in that state to begin with.

I stand and take one last look at her before I head to the bathroom. Hopefully, a shower will clear some of the gaps in my memory and I can go out there armed with some sense of what I might expect when she wakes up. Turning the shower to cold, I hiss as I step under the freezing spray, hoping the ice water can unlock some of the fuzzy memories from my fogged-up brain.

How did I end up here with the woman who has haunted my dreams for so many years naked in my bed? The last thing I remember is drinking with her at the bar as we laughed about all the shit we'd gotten up to in college. As I scrub my body with the shower gel provided by the hotel, I spin the dial to warm my shivering body and, slowly, snippets of memory start to flash behind my eyes.

A flash of Audrey and I at the poker table, her head tipped back with a smile as she raised her fisted hands for my lips, asking me for luck, crosses my brain. Of me kissing her hand and whispering something in her ear that made her blush before she turned and threw the dice, and a cheer as she pulled the chips toward her.

The scene flashes again as water pummels my muscles, and I see her caged between my forearms, her head tipped back. A look of pure lust on her stunning face as her hands grip my shirt. The sweet, succulent taste of her lips on mine and the naked hunger in her eyes. I can practically feel her skin beneath my fingers, but it's all so blurry, like a dream just out of reach. I can almost touch it, but the gaps are taking it further out of my reach the harder I try and hold on to it.

I ache as the ghost of her touch wanders over my skin, my cock aching and stiff against my belly. I fist my length, stroking as a hiss whispers between my teeth. Even the faded, misty memory of Audrey is better than any other sexual experience I've ever had. To think she's just on the other side of that door, naked in my bed, and I haven't got enough memories to piece together exactly what happened between us last night.

Knowing I won't disrespect her by jerking off like an inexperienced and uncontrolled boy, I grab the shampoo and, ignoring my aching dick, begin to wash the smell of stale booze and regret from my hair. As the suds run down my neck, a piercing scream rips through the room. Without thought, I wrench the shower door open and run. My only thought is the sound of anguish coming from Audrey.

I barrel into the suite where Audrey is sitting up in bed, a sheet barely covering her gorgeous body. I'm momentarily held frozen in the grasp of her beauty, as her dark hair falls around her shoulders and her swollen lips tease me with the promise of pure sin, but her eyes are locked on her hand, and I follow her gaze to the huge diamond ring on the third finger of her left hand.

The Enemy

My heart pounds in my chest as I see the princess-cut diamond nestled against a wedding band made from pink diamonds beside it. I can hardly take in what I'm seeing, as her head rises and her deep brown eyes find mine in panic.

"Please tell me we didn't?"

Cold bubbles of shampoo run down my chest, reminding me of my nakedness as I face the only woman I've ever wanted and the only one I ever failed. I want to tell her it will be okay, that we didn't go to the Little White Wedding Chapel last night and make a huge mistake, but I can't. Because every memory from the night before is now blasting me with clear precision.

"Hudson, for fuck's sake, say something!"

I can hear the panic, mixed with anger and something more, something my heart wants to hold on to in the cold harsh light of day. "We did."

I spin on bare feet and walk back into the bathroom, feeling like a fucking failure, my shoulders hunched with shame and defeat. Not for marrying her. I'd marry Audrey in a heartbeat if I knew it was what she wanted, but for taking advantage and there's no doubt that's what I did. I let my heart and what I wanted carry me away. The memories are coming quick and easily now, flooding my brain with clarity as I rinse off my body in the warm rainfall shower.

Of Audrey and me walking into the chapel. Of us saying our vows. Of her giggling and holding onto me as I slid the rings over her knuckles. At some point, I remember a picture being taken and then a sting and buzz. I almost wrench my neck as I turn to look over my shoulder and see the fresh ink on my skin.

There, for all the world to see, is a tiny rose with our initials intertwined among the thorns and leaves surrounding it. Part of me wants to erase every part of what happened last night but there's a small part of me that will never regret what happened. I know Audrey will want this ended and dealt with secretly and cleanly, and I'd never take that from her. She hates me and she's made that very clear. What we shared years ago, and what I did, wounded her in a way she can never forgive me, and I have to live with that.

Pulling a towel around my waist, I brush my teeth and give myself a minute to settle my raging emotions so I can go out there and be the calm, controlled, unemotional bastard that she knows me as now. Pulling open the door, I see her dressed in the outfit from the wedding. Even rumpled and disheveled, she's the most beautiful woman in the world and, for a brief moment, she was mine again, but now I have to do the right thing.

My only relief is that we didn't have sex. Not because I didn't want her, but because I want her more than anything. If I ever get the privilege of touching her like that again, I want her to be fully on board with that, and I can see by the look in her eyes that she isn't right now.

Her anguish cuts a jagged path through my heart, flaying the broken edges, but this isn't about me. It's about making things right and I have the chance to do that now.

I feel her eyes trail over my skin, pricks of heat causing my blood to heat and I know she wants me. I know this attraction between us is real. It's always been real. It's the small hope that keeps me coming back for more of her tongue lashings. It's the tiny kernel of light that, maybe one day, I can earn my way back into her affections. But not like this.

"I'm sorry, Audrey. I make no excuses for my behavior or my lack of control. What I allowed to happen was unforgivable and I'll make sure this mistake is rectified immediately. Nobody needs to know about this."

I see her wince and want to go to her and reassure her that I'll fix this mess, but she isn't mine to comfort.

"Stop with the martyr speech. This is as much on me as it is on you." Audrey rises from the bed and turns her phone to me. "We're trending."

I frown as I take her phone and scan the headlines.

'Kennedy Heiress marries in shock Vegas wedding.'

A picture of the two of us, smiling at the camera, fills the screen and, despite the circumstances, I can't help but wish it were real. I read on, scrolling down the hundreds of comments and new headlines.

'Heiress marries in shotgun wedding. Could there be a bun in the Kennedy oven?'

My lips curl as each sensational headline is tackier than the one before. I glance up as she holds her hand out for her phone and I pass it back, my fingers skimming her palm, electricity arcing between us.

I want more than anything to reach out and pull her into my arms, but she isn't mine and never will be.

3. Audrey

My skin prickles where he touched me, and it takes everything in me not to show him how much he affects me. Standing in front of me like some Greek god, the picture of every fantasy I'd ever had come to life. The dips and curves of his muscled abdomen led to a fine sprinkling of dark hair. The V over his hips pointing down like an arrow to what awaits if I succumb to this wild attraction.

I hate how in control Hudson is as if this dire situation doesn't affect him at all. Just another day in the life of Hudson fucking Carmichael and the proud, almost arrogant tilt of his chin as he watches me. I hate him and yet my eyes continue to dip, wanting to trace every line of his body with my hands, my lips. The distant memory of what we shared digging sharp claws into me and making me remember what we had. Until he broke us.

That thought alone helps snap me from this lust-filled fog. I can never forget. I carry the scars, both physical and mental, because of what he did. I harness that hurt like I always do and allow it to calm me in the face of the situation I find myself.

The Enemy

Having no memory of what happened should scare me, and it does, but what scares me more is that I might have slept with Hudson and have no memory of it. I own my mistakes and if I allowed Hudson to fuck me, I want to remember every delicious second of it. Every orgasm, every cry, and every flex of his body over mine. The direction of my thoughts makes me angry as I see the cocky smirk on his full lips.

I need to get away from this infuriating man before I do something even more stupid than drunk marrying him, and that's to sober fuck him. Mustering up every ounce of the haughty, cutting person I've cultivated over the years, I glance at him, letting disgust curl my lip. "I'm going to take a shower. Can you please have some clothes brought up for me?"

Hudson arches a dark brow at my demand but says nothing, merely dipping his head. How can he be so calm, so controlled in the face of this public shitstorm? I walk away quickly, turning to drown out his addictive intensity. "And can you please put some damn clothes on?" I slam the door with a satisfying snap and hear his laughter on the other side. I lift my hand, wanting to throw something, anything, or scream but my phone in my hand rings, startling me out of my fury.

I groan as I glance at the screen.

Lincoln.

Damn, just what I didn't need. I could let it go to voicemail but, as I already have fifteen missed calls, I decide I might as well get this over with. "Don't start." My defensive response is instinctive as I try to ward off what I know is coming.

"What the fuck, Audrey? You married that prick?"

My eyes roll up to the heavens at my cousin's opening statement of the obvious. "Apparently so."

"What the hell were you thinking?"

A huff leaves my lips at his question, and it's one I wish I had the answer to. "Well, clearly I wasn't fucking thinking, was I?"

My sharp retort is met with silence.

"Did he force you?"

My heart hammered in my chest at Lincoln's question and, as much as I might hate the man on the other side of the door to me, I'd never let anyone think that of him. He was a lot of things, but he wasn't a man who would force a woman. "Of course not. He's an asshole, not a psychopath."

"I just don't want to see him hurt you again, Aud."

My fingers tighten on the sink I'm leaning against, my shoulders relaxing a fraction from the release of tension. Linc was my cousin, but he was also the brother I'd never had. He protected me, and I him, and, when the past between us was woven with poison and pain, Lincoln was the only person who knew even a small part of it.

It was hard for a woman in my position to lean on others, to show weakness of any kind. I always had to be seen as harder, stronger, and less emotional than the men I faced, so showing a softer side was reserved strictly for those few I trusted. Lincoln's words were a reminder that I'm not alone, that people had my back if I allowed it.

My voice softened as I responded. "I know, and I promise you he didn't force anything. This was a drunken mistake, and I'll fix it."

"What do you need from me?"

So typical of my cousin to step up for me. Linc was a hard-faced asshole who didn't show the world his soft side, but when you had his loyalty and love, you had it for life. He'd move heaven and earth for those he cared about.

My thoughts instantly turned to all the ways this news could damage my reputation. My job, my career, the years of working my ass off to garner the respect I deserved. Not because of my family name but because I was damn good at what I did. I knew Lincoln saw me for what I did for Kennedy Enterprises, but that wouldn't stop the old guard from whispering and plotting.

"Can you appease the board? Tell them I'll make a statement about everything and clean this up but keep it vague until I iron out the details with Hudson. I've already had three missed calls from my mother I need to deal with. So, if you could do that, it would be a big help."

A warm chuckle moved down the line. "Yes, I can do that for you. Once you've spoken to your mother and father, my wife is chomping at the bit to speak to you, so be prepared for the inquisition coming your way."

Urgh, just what I need. My friends have been bugging me about Hudson and our history for months and now I'll need to give them something. The thought makes my skin prickle. That pain is still raw around the edges, just ready to cut me if I let it.

"Okay, well, I might need a few hours so hold the fort."

"Will do, cous."

Hanging up, I strip my clothes quickly before stepping into the huge shower. Instantly I'm hit by the scent of Hudson Carmichael. Layers of it surround me like a silky caress, teasing and seducing me as I close my eyes and let the water cleanse me. My eyes pop open as I fight the sensations. Now isn't the time for self-indulgence. I have a mess to clear up. Showering clinically, I shove my wet hair into a ponytail with a band I find in the cupboard under the sink. Wrapping a towel around myself, I survey the damage sleeping with a full face of make-up has done to my skin.

A knock makes me jump and I glare at the door as if it's the sole source of my anger when that's the man behind it. "What?"

"Fresh clothes outside the door."

It's on the tip of my tongue to thank him, but I bite it back. If I give Hudson an inch, he'll take a mile and he doesn't deserve even that small mercy. It's his fault I find myself in this shitty situation. If he'd just left me alone at the bar none of this would have happened. But no, he had to push, he had to get his way and now here we are.

Opening the door, I grab the clothes from the floor and slam the door in his face, garnering a smidgen of satisfaction from the way his eyes went hooded at the sight of me wet and half-naked.

Sorting through the pile in my hands, I find everything I could need, from sleek black trousers from my favorite designer to a silk blouse in a rich, ruby red. Even the underwear was my size and preferred brand. I have no idea how he knows and, right now, I don't want to know either. I need to focus on getting this dealt with and treat it like any other contract negotiation by cutting the emotion out of it. Dressing, I slip my feet into the shoes I wore yesterday and look at myself in the mirror.

I'd kill for my make-up bag, but as I'm not in my suite, but Hudson's, I have to play the hand I was dealt. I pinch my cheeks to add a little color and do my best to wipe the smudges of mascara from under my eyes. It's obviously above his pay grade to include make-up removers when he'd ordered me some clothes. I know the thought was a little unfair and petty of me, but Hudson brings out the worst in me.

Deciding that what I see in the mirror will have to do, I turn and pull open the bathroom door. Hudson is standing with his back to me in the middle of the suite facing the window that overlooks the magnificent Vegas strip. His muscles tense but he doesn't turn around, allowing me a moment to admire his proud stance. Hudson has always been handsome, but that wasn't why I loved him. I loved him because he showed me how I wanted to be loved. How I deserved to be loved. As if I was precious and strong. He held me when I was weak and stood beside me, making me stronger. Until he didn't, until he tore me in a way I've never healed from.

"Nice to see you put some clothes on. Although I fail to see why you need to prance around without a shirt on."

Hudson half turns, his lips flickering in an almost knowing smile that I want to wipe from his face. Instead, I focus on the coffee in his hand. I don't know why I do it, but my feet carry me to his side where I take the cup from him easily and steal the hot, rich brew for myself. It's silly and childish and so far beneath me, but he brings out a side in me I don't recognize as the woman who makes billion-dollar deals every day.

"How could you let this happen, Hudson?"

Attack is my best defense against him until I can get some space and unpack the multitude of feelings flowing through me. I know it's wrong to blame him when we're equally to blame, but I'm not feeling particularly rational right now. Hudson has his hands in the pockets of his joggers as he turns toward me, and I catch sight of his hard nipples. Desire, hot and potent, slides through me, making me want to squeeze my thighs together to garner some relief.

"And what exactly did I let happen, wife?"

A gasp slips out between my lips at the word 'wife'. I once dreamed of him calling me that, of being his in every way, and this disaster makes a mockery of that. "I am *not* your wife." I spit the words as if they offend me and they do, but my reaction only betrays how much I'm affected as I see him smirk.

"Technically, you are my wife, Audrey."

"Technically, I'm a lot of things, including the woman you abandoned."

"Audrey."

I hold up my hand to stop him from speaking and opening up old wounds that have no place in this conversation. "I don't want to talk about it."

Hudson snorts and turns, walking toward the center of the room where his shirt from yesterday lies carelessly over the back of a chair. Discarded and forgotten. "Of course you don't."

My eyes snap to him, and anger fills my chest. "What the fuck does that mean?"

Hudson rounds on me, his face a mask of emotions, each one flitting past so fast I can't keep up before he shakes his head and drops his gaze.

"Forget it."

Half of me wants to push, wants to fight with him, wants to demand to know why he left me, why he did what he did, but the bigger part of me doesn't want to let him know I care enough to have it out.

"Let's just get an annulment and forget this nightmare ever happened."

Pain tightens my abdomen and chest and, for a second, I wonder if I'm having a heart attack. I should probably call Beck and have him check me over but, deep down, I know the source of my pain is the man in front of me. Nobody can inflict a wound on me like he can. "We can't."

I follow his gaze to the bed, rumpled sheets evidence of the night we spent together. I can't remember having sex with him, but I'll never admit it, so I shrug as if it has no effect on me whatsoever. "Fine, a divorce then, and don't think about coming after my fortune or I'll destroy you."

The money means little to me, but I know the wound my words will inflict and I revel in the fleeting look of hurt I see on his face before he masks it. He was always so aware of the differences in our financial circumstances and the whispers people made about us, but it never bothered me. I loved him for who he was, and I knew he was never about my money or wealth. Hudson is a proud man and that is why I knew my barbed comment would land. Yet, as he looks at me with disgust, I feel shame wash over me and have to bite my tongue to keep the apology inside.

"You have nothing I want, Audrey."

"Good, then I'll expect the papers first thing Monday morning."

"I'll see to it."

I nod, nothing left to say, and yet I don't want to leave it like this. I make my way slowly towards the couch and pick up my bag, scanning the area for anything else I might have left, ignoring his presence, and my skin tingles where he watches me.

"For what it's worth, Audrey, I am sorry. I would never have put you in this position on purpose."

Lifting my head, I meet his gaze and see the truth in his words. I know Hudson hurt me, and I know we're broken beyond repair, but I do know he'd never stoop so low as to try and trap me. Tears sting the back of my nose and words are impossible through the thickness of emotion, so I just nod and walk out the door.

Another chapter in our never-ending story of destruction is over

The Enemy

and hopefully, I won't have to see him again. I don't think my heart can take it, and I know my pride can't. I make a quick stop at my apartment so that I can gather myself for the meeting with my parents, not knowing that some chapters are just the prologue to a story I never saw coming.

4. Hudson

WALKING THROUGH THE DOOR OF MY HOME IS LIKE SHEDDING A skin. Some days I feel like I'm two different people—the man the world sees, confident, accomplished, and controlled and then there's the man I am here. I smile as I hear tinkling laughter from the back of the house where the kitchen leads into the den off the side. My home isn't what anyone would expect of me, but it reflects the man I want to be, the man I am for her.

Stepping into the chaos of the den, I see toys and art supplies scattered all over the floor, and a smile pulls at my lips, tension easing from my shoulders. Tia hasn't spotted me yet and it gives me a moment to watch her as she pokes her tongue from between her lips, her grip on the crayon in her hand tight as she concentrates on whatever she's drawing. My heart soars in my chest and my world settles in a kind of restful peace. This is what matters most. Her happiness, her safety from a world that is cruel.

When I look at my baby sister, all I see is her beauty, her infectious laugh, and the unparalleled goodness of her heart. But others don't. They see the way her eyes slant, her nose and profile slightly flatter than most, and note the tell-tale characteristics of Downs Syndrome.

I hate that the world, that purports to be so forward thinking, so evolved, can still be so cruel and judgmental to someone with a heart that is more beautiful than any I've ever known. Protecting Tia has been my number one job since she was placed in my arms the day she was born. I'd fallen in love so hard and fast it, had taken my breath away. I vowed, there and then in that hospital room, to protect her with every breath I had, and to do that, I had to make sacrifices.

I never regretted them, not then and not now, but I have and will always regret the way I handled my situation with Audrey. Hurting her is the biggest regret of my life. The pain I caused her and the words she uses to lash out at me still are my punishment, but, for just a moment in time yesterday, we were together again. A wistful melancholy seeps into me and, for a moment, I wish that things could be different. That my mother could see the beautiful daughter she brought into the world growing up. That Audrey was mine and we were sharing a life together, but it wasn't meant to be.

I know I'm a bastard for letting her believe we slept together when I know, now my head is clearer, and the memories of last night unfettered by alcohol, that we just kissed and messed around before she passed out drunk. I don't know why I lied. No, that's a lie, I do know. I lied because a part of me wants to cling to this moment, this nightmare as she called it, for a little longer and pretend she's mine for a little while before the dream is taken away.

"Huddy."

I snap out of my reverie as Tia runs toward me, a huge grin on her face as she launches her tiny body at me and I catch her in a hug, twirling her off the floor and spinning her until she giggles.

"Have you been a good girl for, Mrs. Price?"

"Yes."

My gaze moves to Mrs. Price as she hefts her body from the chair where she was coloring with Tia and comes toward me. Her movements are slower and pain is etched on her fragile face.

"Arthritis?"

Mrs. Price has been with us from day one. My mother's old neighbor, she loved my mom like a daughter and, when I was left a young, single caretaker of a child with special needs, she stepped in to help me. As a retired kindergarten teacher, she's familiar with what kids need, more so than I will ever be and I'd be lost without her.

"Age comes with a price, Hudson, but one I'm happy to pay."

"Is there anything I can do to help?" Guilt rides me hard, knowing I need to stop relying on her so much, but I'm a selfish prick and I don't want to upset the balance with Tia. She loves Mrs. Price like a grandmother and replacing her will break Tia's heart and my own.

"Nope, nothing you can do. I just have to soldier through." She turns to Tia and palms her cheek, the love she feels for my baby sister clear on her face. "Time with this angel is all I need to distract me."

"I was good, wasn't I?"

A warm smile reaches the older woman's cheeks as Tia cuddles into my chest. Burrowing into me like a koala. "You were an angel, as usual. Although you could do with eating more of those veggies I give you."

"I don't like trees, though."

I roll my lips under my teeth to stop the smile as Tia pouts.

"That may be so, but they're good for you."

Trees are what Tia calls broccoli, and she isn't a fan, at least not anymore. She was when she was younger, but now everything seems to change on a daily basis, and I struggle to keep up. I wonder if other parents feel as out of their depth as me most days or if I'm just fundamentally not cut out for this.

"Mrs. Price is right, you need to eat your veggies. You know what the doctor said."

Tia sighs. "I need to be big and strong so I can go to school like the other kids."

I fight the smile at her sulky frown before she smiles wide and pushes away from my chest, wanting to be let down. I release her and hate that these moments are getting fewer and farther between. Tia is growing into her own amazing person and it's what I want. I want her to experience life and all its beauty, to be independent and achieve everything I know she can, but it wars with my need to protect her and shelter her from the horror of the world.

"I drew you."

"You did?"

I crouch as she runs back to her desk and then returns, her pigtails bobbing as she runs, a colorful drawing of a man with an extra arm sticking out the side of his neck, a pink tie, a gray suit, and blue hair. A little girl with a crown atop her head holding his hand. Her skills are still behind other children of her age, but she's making progress day by day. Tia has the fight of a warrior and when I think back to all she's had to go through in her young life, all she's lost, I'm astounded and humbled by her.

"I love it."

"Can we put it on the fridge?"

I stand and purse my lips, shaking my head. I watch her face fall before I speak. "I think this needs pride of place in my home office."

Tia's face beams as she throws herself into my arms.

"I love you, Huddy."

I kiss her hair, relishing the scent of strawberry shampoo, which I've used on her hair since she was a baby. This is home for me; Tia and the unquestionable love she gives me. This is what matters. "Love you, too."

I stand, fighting the emotion that doesn't usually leave me so raw, and walk Mrs. Price to the door while Tia dances around the den, playing some imaginary game in her head.

She stops me at the door. "I saw what happened in Vegas."

My jaw clenches, any hope of hiding my misdemeanor is gone. "I guess what happened in Vegas doesn't stay in Vegas after all."

Mrs. Price ignores my attempt at humor. "That's her, isn't it?"

My muscles still and I want to deny it, but this woman knows me too well. Yet still I don't confirm her words. "What makes you say that?"

"Look at the picture that Fresh News is running."

She leaves me with those cryptic words, and I watch her amble slowly down the drive and get into the five-year-old Toyota she won't let me replace before she drives away. Taking out my phone, I scroll to Fresh News and don't even have to bother searching for the article about Audrey and I and our impromptu marriage because it's front and center. I curse my stupidity. I know better than to let something like this happen.

I click on the thumbnail of an image and instantly my heart constricts in my chest, sweat dotting my brow, because even a blind person could see how I feel about Audrey from this picture.

Audrey is beaming at the camera, but my eyes are on her, and every tender feeling I have for her is shining in my eyes. I don't know what possessed me to allow myself to be open like I did, but I need to get a lid on this and fast. A quick divorce contract should be simple enough to draft after Tia is in bed, but today I want to spend the day with my favorite person in the world.

A DAY SPENT PLAYING OUTSIDE IN THE SUNSHINE WITH TIA WAS just what I needed. Everything is simple when I block out the noise and simply let myself enjoy my time with her. It's not something I get to do as often as I'd like, and I know she misses me. Tia doesn't hide her feelings or thoughts from me and it's refreshing, but also brutal sometimes when I see how my absence affects her.

We play ball in the park, kicking it between us gently as she asks me question after question about everything, from why trees can't talk to if I've ever met a real mermaid. It's exhausting and wonderful, and the innocence of it is the perfect balm. We get lunch at Tia's favorite pizza place and eat ice cream down by the pier as she looks for mermaids. Her constant chatter is a perfect counter to my thoughts, keeping me from obsessing over the last twenty-four hours.

The Enemy

I ignore the constant calls from Lincoln Coldwell and the few I've received from Ryker Cabot. The latter I might consider a friend, but I know how protective Audrey's friends are of her and I love that she has that. I ignore them all. This is between Audrey and I and, no matter how much they care, it's none of their business.

A text pops through from Lottie Coldwell and I smile. Lottie is Lincoln's wife and, for better or worse, she worships him. I drew up the original contract between them, which was a marriage of convenience, in effect to get her out of a whole lot of debt. At the time, I thought she was making a huge mistake, but in hindsight, it was for the best. They got their happy ending, even if it did have a whole lot of heartbreak on the way. I respect Lottie and what she was willing to do for her brother who has diabetes. I saw a lot of myself in her and our stories had a similarity that made me want to help her.

We were both raising our siblings after our mothers' deaths and fighting the uphill battle of that twisting road. It took me a while to really see how much Lincoln loved her, and I still wouldn't say I like the man, but I tolerate him because I consider Lottie a friend. Even if she doesn't have any knowledge of Tia's existence.

Nobody does. I keep my private life locked down so tightly that nobody knows about her. Not because I'm ashamed, but to protect her from the people I work for and with. Also, because I hoard that happy part of my life like a dragon and his gold. It's mine and I want to protect it. I don't want the outside to corrupt my sanctuary.

I open the text as Tia skips along beside me, singing some song from a movie about an Ice Princess.

LOTTIE: YOU HAVE SOME SERIOUS EXPLAINING TO DO, MISTER.

I laugh out loud at the tame threat in her tone. I'll respond later once Tia is asleep.

I drive us home and make a light dinner of fruit salad before I commence the bedtime routine I have in place for Tia. Once bathing is done and teeth are cleaned, I sit on the edge of her pink bed as she rests against me and read her favorite story, pausing on each page so that she can run her fingers over the pictures she knows by heart. As her body slides into sleep, I continue reading, this familiar routine soothing to me, too.

Closing the book, I tuck the blanket around my sister and kiss her dark curly head. She's so much like my mother, and I'm glad for it. She has nothing of the bastard that sired her, in looks or personality.

I'm picking up the toys from the den floor when my phone vibrates with a text. Expecting it to be another voicemail message I frown, but it's not a voicemail. It's a message from Audrey.

I NEED TO SEE YOU.

Not what I was expecting after the way we parted today, but not unwanted either. I'll always be an addicted fool for Audrey Kennedy.

TOMORROW IN MY OFFICE? SAY TEN AM?

The response is instant like she was holding her phone in her hand waiting for my reply. The thought causes a thrill to shoot up my spine.

I NEED TO SEE YOU IN PRIVATE, AS SOON AS POSSIBLE. TONIGHT? I COULD COME TO YOU?

I hesitate, not wanting to break that barrier between home and work, but then, that ship has sailed as I'm married to the woman texting me. Tia is in bed and never wakes once she's out, so I won't have to deal with explaining who Audrey is to Tia.

FINE. SAY AN HOUR. I'LL SEND YOU MY ADDRESS.

NO NEED. I HAVE IT.

Fucking Ryker and his nosey ass snooping.

FINE.

I want to say more, I want to ask her what this is about, what's so important, but I also know that Audrey will only tell me when she's ready. Yet I sense an urgency in her texts, which is unusual for her.

I tidy up, my mind playing over every memory from last night as they become clearer and clearer. Touching her, kissing her, holding her hand. Her suggesting we just get hitched and fuck the consequences. I knew at the time, still lucid enough for her comment to bring me up short, that it was a bad idea. But as she took my hand and dragged me to the nearest jeweler, her hand warm in mine, the hot honey of her laughter coating my skin, I let myself get carried away.

I knew the moment I saw that princess-cut diamond it would be perfect for her, and the pink diamond wedding band was everything I remembered about Audrey the girl. Delicate, glamorous, and, despite the pink color, classy.

Deciding that, if left alone, the next forty-five minutes will be spent pacing and overthinking, I head to my office to draw up the papers in case she wants them tonight.

I open my laptop and see a message from Cutter Hendrix, my sort of private detective, stroke, fixer. Opening the email, I see the attachment and the words *this is what you need.*

My heart beats faster as I open the attachment and see the file with all the incriminating data I need to take this bastard down. Smiling, I take the burner phone from my locked drawer and hit dial on the only number in the phone. It rings twice before a voice answers.

"It must be important if you're calling me on your honeymoon, Carmichael. A woman like that in my bed, and I wouldn't be seen for weeks."

It takes every ounce of control I have not to react to his words, but I know a reaction is what he's looking for. That and information. "You know me, old friend, I'm not one to let anything get in the way of the work we do."

A deep baritone chuckle peels down the line and I wait. I hate myself for talking about Audrey like she doesn't matter, but he can't know who she is to me or what she means. He'll use it to manipulate me. That is just who he is, who I am in some ways. But we're not alike, we just have the same focus.

Lorenzo Abruzzo is head of the Italian Mafia, and I'm the lowly lawyer who dragged himself from the slums, but we have a common goal. To take down as many men who hurt women as we can, whether that's by helping the women start new lives away from abuse, or by removing the problem.

That is our only commonality. I don't work for him, and I have nothing to do with his business or personal life, but we both lost women we love to abusive men. It's why he fought to take over as the head of his family, killing family members to do so, and why I lead this double life, walking a fine line between law-abiding and law-breaking.

"And very sweet distraction, I suspect."

"I have the file we need." I change the subject, focusing on the reason for the call and steering it away from Audrey.

"Oh, and what does it say?"

"This one is bad. He got the girl pregnant and, when she told him she was pregnant, he had her killed."

Lorenzo swears in Italian, his hatred for men Like Fletcher Stubbins is almost as vicious as mine.

"How do you wish to play this, Lorenzo?"

My personal preference is to end the man's pitiful life, but he has a wife and daughter who adore him, and, by all accounts, he treats them well. Which is more common than I would've thought when I began this crusade.

"Your way. If I change my mind, I can have him dealt with on the inside."

"As you wish. I'll send the file to the Feds, and they can deal with him."

When we fell into this vigilante crusade over five years ago, we agreed that, if they could be handled legally, we'd do that, and I'd do that part. If the only route was to end their miserable lives, Lorenzo handled it. He's hungrier for blood than me. I just want justice in whatever form it takes and ultimately the women to be safe.

"Good. You can go back to enjoying your wife now, Carmichael."

"Yes, I will."

"We should do lunch. I'd love to meet her."

"Not a fucking chance, Abruzzo. I'd rather stick my dick in a meat grinder than let you near a woman that belongs to me."

I'm staking a claim I don't have, in a way that makes my skin crawl, but it's the only way to ensure he leaves Audrey alone. Not that I fear for her safety, but I know the effect she has on men, and Lorenzo would stop at nothing if he thought he could have a woman like Audrey. I wouldn't put it past her to go out with him just to spite me.

"Point taken. Goodnight, Carmichael."

I hang up and delete the email, ensuring there's no evidence of it on my computer. I haven't technically done anything wrong in the eyes of the law, at least not in any way that can be traced back to me, but I have got my hands dirty. I know the blood on my hands will never wash away and I'm okay with that. The stain on my soul is mine to carry.

An alert on my phone lets me know I have a visitor at the gate, and I scan the camera and see Audrey's Audi RS. Pressing the button to let her in, I move to the door and wrench it open to wait for her. She rounds the corner too fast, gravel kicking up on my drive and I frown, irritated with her for not taking proper care. I'm about to tear into her for it when her car door opens, and I see her step out still wearing the clothes I'd had brought up from the store in the hotel. But what really catches my attention is the utter devastation on her beautiful face.

"Audrey?"

I'm walking before I even realize what I'm doing, grasping her forearms to steady her as she looks up at me on the doorstep and a sob of absolute anguish falls from her. I don't think, I just take her in my arms and hold her as she falls apart and vow to do whatever it takes to fix whatever it is that made her cry.

5. Audrey

I lift my head from Hudson's chest as he swipes my tears with his thumbs, and a sense of safety comes over me. I feel like my world is falling apart. I was handling the news I received earlier until I saw him, and then everything was just too much. I knew as I fell apart, he'd catch me.

"Come inside and let's talk."

I nod as he releases me and follow him inside, my eyes darting around like a thief taking in every detail of his home. It isn't what I expected at all. I thought it would be cold with lots of white, clinical minimalism, but it is homey, warm, and inviting.

"Why don't we talk in the lounge?"

I grip my purse and follow him down the hallway, trying to catch peeks of the rooms we pass. The floor is midtone hardwood, the walls differing shades of cream, and the lounge, when we reach it, faces into a large back garden with a pool. Deep couches in soft fabrics face an elegant fireplace and I see a line of pictures on the mantel, but I'm not close enough to see who is in them.

"Sit, please. Would you like a drink?"

"Water, if you don't mind."

The Enemy

I let my gaze wander around the room as Hudson hurried off to get me some water. I don't know why I came here first, but it was instinctive. The conversation with my parents spins around in my head and I try to fight the choking feeling, forcing tears to drown me.

"Darling, we're so happy to see you."

My mother's warm embrace drives the guilt home even further as she leads me into the den where my father, retired judge, John Jones, is sitting in his favorite chair by the window.

"Pumpkin." His wide smile is comforting as he opens his arms and I walk into them. I am, and have always been, a daddy's girl. My father is the man who I measure all men by and only one ever came close.

"Hey, Daddy."

My mother bustled in with a tray filled with coffee and cake and placed it on the table next to my father.

"Where is your young man?"

I pause at my father's question, the coffee cup shaking slightly in my hand. I hate that I have disappointed them, that I'd bring shame on them in any way.

"Mom, Dad, I'm sorry."

My father raises his hand and then glances across at my mother, who has tears in her eyes. I feel an undercurrent of tension and hate that I'm the cause.

"Sweetheart, please, it's okay. Your mother and I know that sometimes, in the heat of the moment, these things happen. I can't say it isn't a bit of a surprise, but you only have to look at the pictures to see how much he loves you."

I make a strangled sound in my throat at my father's words, but he continues before I can correct him.

"The truth is, sweetheart, it's a relief to see you settled with someone. It isn't the way I would've wanted but it makes me happy to know you have someone to support you."

The tone of my father's voice causes a sudden tension in my belly. His speech has an end-of-days quality about it that sets my teeth on edge.

"I have support. I have you and my friends. Why would me marrying Hudson make a difference?"

My mother lets out a sob and I go to her, crouching at her feet and taking her hands in mine. I look at her properly now and see the dark circles around her eyes. The pale translucent quality of her skin. It's so at odds with the classy, glamorous woman I've known all my life.

"Mom, tell me what's going on?"

She looks at me, her eyes shimmering with tears, and then to my father and shakes her head. "I can't. I can't say it, John."

My father pats her hand and nods. "It's okay. It will be alright."

My heart is almost beating out of my chest now, panic holding me in its crippling claws. "Will someone please tell me what's going on?"

"I have cancer."

The bottom of my world falls away at my father's words. Unnatural silence fills the room and I'm sure my heart is going to pound right out of my chest. I shake my head as I sit back on my heels, all the energy wiped out of me like someone has pulled the plug.

"No." I shake my head as if denying the words will make them go away.

My dad reaches for my hands, and I let him take them, a sense of panic filling me, like I need to go back and undo something but it's too late.

"Sweetheart, listen to me. I have stage three Myeloma, which is a type of blood cancer."

"But how? When?"

I stare at the man who has been my rock, the man who I always look to when things are too much, who dries my tears and doesn't ask questions.

"We found out a few weeks ago. I've been getting a few chest infections, so they did some blood work."

"Are you going to die, Daddy?"

My father cups his big hands over my cheeks and looks at me with a ferocious, yet tender gaze. "We're all going to die, Audrey, but my prognosis suggests I have about six months to a year."

The Enemy

That isn't enough. I'm not ready to lose my father. I never will be. I want him to be there for all my highs, to watch me conquer every dream I ever had.

"We have time, sweetheart, but it does mine and your mother's heart good to know you have the love of a good man."

"What?"

"Hudson. Your husband."

Shame coils inside me as I realize that I've robbed my father out of walking me down the aisle. I have to tell them it's all a lie and break their hearts when they're already battling with this. As I go to admit the truth, that my marriage is a drunken shame, I find myself doing the exact opposite. "He is a good man. I love him and he loves me. I can't wait for you to meet him."

As the lie leaves my mouth, I try not to acknowledge how much truth might be in my loving him, because it's a wound that would tear me apart if I opened my heart to it right now.

"We can't wait to meet him either, sweetheart. Maybe you can bring him over for dinner this week. We'd really like to get to know our new son-in-law. Even if he didn't come with you today."

My father's frown makes me smile. He wants what's best for me, but he'll definitely give Hudson a hard time for letting me face this alone as he sees it.

"He had to see a client. You know what it's like, Daddy. The law stops for no man or woman."

"I do. Now, why don't you tell us all about him."

"Audrey."

I blink and look up at Hudson, who is holding a glass of water out to me. I take it with a shaking hand and offer him a small smile.

"Thank you."

Hudson sits opposite me, elbows on his knees, his hands hanging between his thick thighs. He looks different here, relaxed in a way I've never seen.

"What's going on, Aud?"

"My father has cancer." Just saying the words makes me want to vomit all over the floor.

He moves to reach for me and then stops himself, seemingly not sure what to do. We're both a little lost in how to act.

"I'm so sorry. What can I do?"

That right there is the man I fell in love with. He doesn't try and console me or ask me a hundred questions that I can't face right now. He just asks what he can do to help me. I hate that he can still be that man and the man who broke me. It makes hating him so much harder.

I draw myself up, placing the glass on the side table, and try and channel my inner badass. I can't show him weakness even if he does have the upper hand in this situation. His lips twitch as if he can see the shift in me, and desire buzzes in the air around us.

"You can stay married to me."

His eyebrow quirks, giving him a rakish appearance, but I can handle this man easier than the kind one who let me fall apart in his arms.

"And how does that work exactly?"

"My father has six months to a year to live. We stay married and trot out a few appearances for my parents to keep them happy."

"And why would you marrying me in Vegas have made them happy?"

I tuck my hands beneath my bag so he doesn't see the slight tremor. "My father is old-fashioned in some ways and I'm his baby girl. He thinks having a man beside me will make his passing easier for me."

"I see."

I'm not sure he does. How could he possibly understand?

"And why would he think the man who broke his daughter's heart in college is that man?"

I suck in a sharp breath at his words. This is the closest we've come to talking about what happened and it catches me by surprise. I focus on my breathing and look up to see Hudson watching me, an expression I can't read on his handsome face.

"He doesn't know about college."

"So, you propose we remain married and live a lie until he passes and then get a quiet divorce?"

"Yes."

"And what do I get out of this?"

I knew he couldn't do it just to be a good human being. Somehow that makes it easier. The thought of it being transactional is better than owing this man anything. "What is it you want?"

Hudson stands and walks to the fireplace, his broad back to me. He's a fine specimen, with broad shoulders, narrow hips, and, God, the rest of him is perfect too. The image of him naked and wet from this morning is etched on my eyelids. The fact I can remember every moment that has passed between us even after all these years should be an indication of how dangerous this is to my mental health. He could eviscerate me, but if it makes my father's final months happy then I'll walk through the fires of hell for him.

Hudson spins around and pins me with his gaze. "I want weekly dates. I want you to get to know me, to let me show you who I am now, without the sins of my past standing between us like a mating chasm."

I freeze. What he's asking, on the face of it, seems easy, but spending time with him is dangerous. He reeled me in before, with his charisma and charm, and I fell so hard it took me years to even get back up. Yet, I'm not the same woman anymore. I'm stronger, harder, colder and I'll remain so. If he thinks he can win me over with a few dates, he's sadly mistaken. "Fine."

"And nobody can know this is a lie. Not Lincoln. Not anyone."

"Don't be ridiculous. We can't keep a secret like that."

Hudson smirks and shoves a hand in the pocket of his faded jeans, and I wonder if I'll even get out of here without tackling him to the ground and demanding he fuck me. I might hate him, but the effect he has on my body is undeniable.

"Of course we can. You move in here and have your own room and live your life. All I ask is that you give me one night a week to spend time with me."

I look at him incredulously. "I'm not moving in here."

Hudson shrugs one powerful shoulder. "Then I'll draw up the divorce papers."

"Have you not got a decent bone in your body? A good man would do this out of kindness to a dying man."

"We both know I'm not a good man, Audrey."

"You were once." I regret the words the second they slip past my lips.

Hudson prowls towards me, stopping so close I can feel the heat from his body burning through the silk of my blouse.

"That boy is gone. You married the man, so either take the fucking deal or leave."

"Asshole," I hiss.

Tension fills the room until I'm sure the slightest spark will see the room erupt in flames. I don't know whether I want to kiss him or punch him, and he looks to be having similar feelings.

His eyes drop to my lips, and my breasts heave, my fingers itching to touch him, to enact that which I can't remember from last night.

"Huddy?"

My eyes snap to the little girl who is standing at the entrance to the living room, a teddy hanging from her fingers.

Hudson rushes to her and crouches down. "Hey, princess, what are you doing up?"

I watch, my heart twisting in anguish as he scoops her up into his arms as if she's the most precious thing in the world. Pain is like a whip against my skin as I watch her nuzzle close, his hand stroking her soft curls. I know without a doubt this is the baby I saw that night and it breaks me all over again.

Hudson turns to me, watching me carefully and the child lifts her head. I try my best to control my reaction as I see the tell-tale signs of her Down's syndrome.

The Enemy

"You're pretty."

God, she's beautiful. If joy and light had a face, it would be this child. It radiates from her like a beacon in the dark of night. I smile and take a step toward her. "So are you, sweetheart."

This child represents my pain and yet all I feel is warmth for her.

"Audrey, this is Tia. Tia, this is Audrey. She's going to be living with us for a little while. Isn't that right, Audrey?"

My gaze flashes to his and I see the trap as the door closes on me. I look back to the child watching me and don't know if I can handle being so close to my past. It feels like everything is colliding and I might end up collateral damage. Yet, what choice do I have? I came here to do this for my father, a man who's loved me my whole life and a man who looks at me like Hudson is looking at Tia. Like she's his whole world and I know I won't let my father down. "Yes, Huddy, that's right."

He smirks at the name. "How about you come to my office tomorrow and we iron out the details?"

"Or you come to my office?"

It's a silly power play, but I won't let him have all the power in this situation. Hudson beams a smile at me then and my breath catches in my throat. God, I'd forgotten how beautiful he was when he really smiled.

"Perfect. I'll see you then."

"On second thoughts, I'll come to you." I can't have him thinking things are easy.

Hudson walks me to the door, Tia sleepy in his arms, but as we stop in the entryway, Tia reaches out for me with her arms. I look to Hudson, who is watching closely, like he'll step in at a moment's notice and annihilate anyone who doesn't react in a favorable way to her.

"Night-night."

I embrace her awkwardly from where she's still in Hudson's arms, the position making me stumble. Hudson wraps his arm around my waist until we're in a three-way hug. Tia's arms hold tight, and she buries her head in my hair. God, has anything ever felt so innocently perfect? I want to wrap her up and fight battles for this child and I barely even know her.

We pull away and I stroke her cheek. "Goodnight, Princess Tia. Sweet dreams."

"Goodnight, Princess Belle."

My eyes dart to Hudson, who looks as shocked and affected as me. The name he always called me sticks in my belly like a sword.

"I'll see you tomorrow."

I need to get out of there to lick my wounds and regroup before I do or say something I might regret.

As I drive away, I see Hudson close the front door and a breath leaves me. Today has been a month of Mondays. I got married, found out my father was dying, and met the child who took Hudson from me. I have so many feelings right now that I can't process even one of them. I just need to go home. Bury myself in my bed with my favorite caramel praline ice cream and have a good cry.

Tomorrow I can get back to being the Audrey everyone knows and loves.

6. Hudson

I'M SITTING BEHIND MY DESK, TRYING NOT TO WATCH THE CLOCK when I hear a commotion in reception. Standing, I move to the door and pull it open to find Audrey facing down my secretary, Grace.

"I don't need an appointment. I'm his wife."

My dick hardens at her words, and I fight the smile. Something I do a lot around Audrey.

The two warring women haven't even noticed me, and I lean against the door frame and enjoy it for a second. Not two women fighting over me, that gets tired really quick, but Audrey fighting for, or over, me is like fucking Viagra.

"Don't be ridiculous. Hudson would have told me if he'd gotten married."

Audrey is dressed for business this morning in a red pencil skirt that molds around her hips, showcasing her perfect ass, and flaring at her knees, making her long-toned legs look like a fucking honey trap. A black sheer blouse with long sleeves and a high neck gives the illusion of modesty but my mind sees all the tiny buttons and hears them ping to the ground as I tear it from her. Sky-high black heels with red soles complete her look.

"Hudson doesn't tell his staff everything."

"I'm not just staff."

I step forward as Audrey looks ready to throw my secretary out of the window.

"Ladies."

Both turn to me, Audrey breathing fire and Grace looking smug as if I'm going to throw Audrey out. It won't be the first time a woman has come here and tried some underhanded tactic to see me.

"Grace, this is my wife, Audrey. As I'm sure you know from the papers." I give her a reprimanding look because I know she's playing games. Grace is the best secretary I've ever had but she's made it clear on more than one occasion that she'd like more. I've made it just as clear it won't happen but still, she tries to push the boundaries.

"I don't read gossip rags."

Her sulky pout irritates me, but seeing her get under Audrey's skin makes me wonder if my wife might be a smidge jealous.

"Maybe you should and then you won't make a fool of yourself." Audrey sweeps past me on those words, and I get swept up in her scent.

I lean down to Grace and make sure she knows I'm not joking. "In future, if my wife visits, unless I'm with a client, she has full access to me. Is that clear?"

"Yes, Mr. Carmichael."

"Good."

I walk back into my office and close the door, adjusting my cuffs as I turn to find Audrey sitting behind my desk. She looks fierce and fucking stunning. Everything in me wants to fall at her feet and worship her, but that isn't the man she needs right now. She needs control, and fighting with me and winning a hard-fought battle will give her that.

"Unless you want to sit in my lap and have this discussion, I suggest you move."

Audrey snorts. "Like I'd let you near me."

I arch my brow in a mocking statement, and she curls her lip but stands and moves to the window. Looking out over the view of Manhattan, I allow myself a moment to take her in. Her shoulders are high with tension, and she looks like she's lost weight even in the last two days.

"Tell me about your father."

Audrey crosses her arms and spins on her heel to glare at me. "What's there to say? He's dying."

I know it's not that simple. Losing a parent rarely is. "Are there any treatments he can try or trials he can apply for?"

Audrey draws in a shuddering breath but doesn't falter. "No. He has late-stage Myeloma, a type of blood cancer. Apparently, it was symptomless for a long time so, by the time they found it, it had already spread."

"I'm sorry."

Her shoulders bounce as she tries to give a nonchalant shrug, but I know this woman better than I know anyone and she's hurting. Anger suffuses me. How can the world be so cruel to some and then let evil bastards get away scot-free?

"That's life, right?"

"Even so, it sucks. I've met your dad a couple of times in the courtroom and found him to be a good, fair man."

"Thank you."

Audrey rolled her bottom lip between her teeth, making desire race through me. God, would I ever not want her?

"So, I answered your questions. Are you going to tell me about Tia? Why does nobody know about her?"

Tia is such a delicate subject for me and talking about her isn't something I do often, my need to protect her is so ingrained in me but Audrey deserves the truth.

"Tia is the reason I get up in the morning. The reason I work my ass off." I walk toward the coffee machine at the bar in my office and hold a cup up to her in invitation, but she shakes her head. I don't need the caffeine, but I need a minute to get my words together.

"Where is her mother?"

"She died when Tia was six months old." The words are matter of fact but the pain of losing my mother still cuts deep, like a wound that never quite heals. My anchor is gone, and I miss her every day.

"So, you've been alone with her all this time?"

Leaning against the coffee bar, I regard the woman who has always been the one who got away and nod. "Yep, just the two of us. We have some help, but mostly it's just me and her."

"You must really love her."

Her voice is soft as she speaks but I can hear the hurt in her words and wonder why my loving Tia would hurt her so much. "She is everything to me. I'd gladly sacrifice everything I have for her." I don't add that I already had when I left her.

"It can't be easy."

I huff a humorless laugh. Everyone assumes a child with Downs is a burden when the truth is she's my biggest gift in this life. Yet I don't think Audrey means it that way. "Being a caretaker is never easy, but Tia makes it easier in some ways. She has this goodness about her, this light and joy. She sees the world differently. I just wish the world saw her with the same joy." Disappointment in the world is a heavy burden sometimes.

I see Audrey frown. "That's a funny turn of phrase."

I cock my head in question, not sure what she means. "What is?"

"Caretaker. Surely it would be easier to say 'father'?"

I push off the console and prowl toward her. Fighting the pull this woman has on me is almost impossible. "Perhaps but I'm not her father, so I don't wish to confuse the issue."

Audrey seems to pale before my eyes and I step closer instinctively as she stumbles back, my hand lifting and hesitating just an inch from touching her, not sure if I should but wanting it more than my next breath.

"You're not?"

I frown confused, unsure why this news seems to affect her so hard. "No, of course not. Tia is my baby sister."

"She is?"

The Enemy

Sudden realization hits me hard. "Yes. What? Did you think she was my daughter?"

I can't get my head around why she'd think that. Tia being mine would form the assumption that I'd cheated on Audrey. As if a boulder had landed on my chest, I struggle to breathe. I blink and step back, watching her incredulously, appalled that she'd believe that. "Wait, you think I cheated on you?"

Audrey folds her arms over her chest, causing my eyes to drop to the swells that I itch to feel against my palms. Her walls are coming up fast in front of my eyes, the tilt of her mouth determined and angry. "I'm not here to discuss the past."

I want to argue, to defend myself, but I know I need to be smart, to let her come to the realization on her own. Audrey has spent a long time hating me and thinking I cheated so it will take a little while for her to switch that anger off and allow herself to even consider she might be wrong about what happened.

"Fine. Let's discuss this little plan of yours then."

"Good. I propose we stay married. I'll stay at your house at the weekends and at my apartment during the week. Nobody will suspect because it's closer to the city and I often have late meetings at the club."

"Alright. I want you at my house Friday to Monday when we can travel together."

Her lips thin but she nods and I bite back the smile of triumph. Every little victory with Audrey is hard won and all the sweeter for it.

"I also want you to meet my parents and act accordingly."

"You mean like I worship the ground you walk on?"

"Exactly."

Little does she know that will be the easy part. I've loved her since the day we met and not a day in between has that love faded, but I can't tell her that now. She'd reject it and build her walls even higher to keep me out. "Then I want the same in front of your friends. I won't come out of this looking like some poor schmuck so desperate to do your bidding that I'll sacrifice my pride."

Audrey sniffs. "I can't do that. I don't lie to my friends."

"Okay, we can compromise on that. You can tell your close friends, the club owners, and their wives. Anyone else will think you're hanging on my every word like a lovesick teenager but I want one extra night at my house."

I watch her shoulders stiffen and think I might have pushed too hard, but I won't back down. No matter how much I love her, I can't be weak. She doesn't respect weak people and I'm too arrogant and stubborn to let her walk all over me. Unless she's naked in six-inch heels, then I might reconsider my stance.

"I haven't ever been a lovesick teenager and I agree to the extra night."

"Oh, please. We both know that's a lie."

I fold my arms over my chest to stop myself from reaching for her and hauling her into my arms. She conceded easier than I thought on the extra night and something about her submission gives me the primal urge to kiss her until she's boneless and begging for my cock.

"Do we? As I remember it, we had decent sex and a few laughs. It was never serious."

I almost laugh at her blatant attempt to minimize what we had. "Bullshit. What we had was real. In fact, it was damn near perfect. And the sex was never decent, it was fucking life-changing, so don't lie to yourself or me."

"If it was so perfect, you wouldn't have walked away so easily, so save me the melodramatics."

"I thought we weren't talking about the past, Audrey?"

"We're not but we are talking about sex."

"Are we?"

"Yes."

I love this back-and-forth with her. This is Audrey at her best. She could cut you with her sharp tongue, and outsmart anyone I know with her whiplash intellect, but underneath she's soft, loving, and I want her back in my life for good. "Okay."

"While we're together, I demand discretion. If you want to get your dick wet, you make sure nobody finds out and I don't see it. I won't be the butt of people's jokes."

I feel all the humor at our verbal sparring wither away and die. Fury is churning in my gut now, that she'd believe I'd do that to her, that I'd disrespect her in such a way.

I stalk closer and spear my hand through her soft tresses, tilting her face to mine and speaking so close my lips brush her pouty bottom lip. God, the taste of her is right there for the taking. Her hands find my chest to steady herself from my sudden invasion, but she shows no fear, as she shouldn't. I'd cut off my own dick before I'd hurt her. No, what I see is a hundred times more dangerous.

I see my own wants and needs mirrored in her wild, slumberous eyes. Her body shifts, softening against me and my cock pushes against the zipper of my pants to break free. I'm so damn hard for her it's painful.

"Let's get a few things straight right here and now. First, I would never disrespect you by cheating on you, no matter what you think of me. Second, if I want to get my dick wet, I'll be getting wet inside my wife's gorgeous cunt or silky, sinful mouth."

A sharp inhale of breath has me fighting back a groan but, as much as she wants to submit to me, Audrey is fighting it and it will only make it sweeter when she eventually succumbs, and we both know she will. We're destined.

"You bring that dick anywhere near me, I'm going to bite it off."

A husk of laughter bubbles out of me at her words and my fist tightens in her hair as I see pleasure and pain wash over her features. "So that's your kink."

"I don't have a kink."

"Liar."

Audrey flushes and I want to kiss her so bad it's like a siren song in my blood.

"I hate you."

I release her then, stepping away before I do something I'll regret, like bending her over my desk and fucking her until she admits she still wants me as badly as I want her.

"For the record, Audrey, I don't share. So while we're married, you don't fuck anyone else. If you have needs, you come to me, and I'll look after you."

Her cheeks pink, and a sudden memory of her smiling up at me in bed, her naked body relaxed against mine as we whispered and planned a future we thought would be very different from the one we have hits me. Her pert nipples, the same shade as the blush on her cheeks, rub against the cotton of my shirt. I clench my fist as the need to bury myself into her body makes my cock ache.

"No need, I have a collection of toys that can get the job done better than any man."

She's lying. She came so hard when we fucked I thought campus security were going to knock the door down, but I let her have her lie for now.

"What are your other demands?"

"I need to know Kennedy is safe. I know I fucked up on Saturday but I don't want the company my family built put in jeopardy when we divorce."

"Have the paperwork drawn up and I'll sign it."

"Thank you."

I nod at the relief in her voice, not trusting myself to say more as I release her and step away.

Audrey twists her fingers around each other in a rare sign of nerves before she speaks next. "What about Tia?"

My shoulders tense. "What about her?"

"What will you tell her?"

"We'll tell her a version of the truth. You're my wife, and you'll be living with us some of the time."

"Won't that confuse things?"

I shake my head. "Tia will just accept you. It's who she is. She adapts better than most." I feel my lips pull at the edges as I remember Tia's chatter this morning about Princess Belle. I can't help but wonder if it's because we're half-siblings that we see the same thing in Audrey or if it's because it's the book I read to her the most.

"I'll follow your lead with her then."

My head comes up as she moves toward my desk. I watch her, waiting until she makes eye contact, and let the emotions I have regarding Tia show on my face. Tia is my greatest gift but also my biggest vulnerability and I need Audrey to understand that I mean business about this. "Just don't hurt her. I've spent my life protecting her and I won't have her hurt because of my own stupid actions, not for you and not for anyone else, either. She's my priority and always will be."

I see her flinch, but Audrey holds her head up straight like a Queen in waiting. I don't want to hurt her, ever, but I need her to know that Tia is the line I won't let anyone cross.

"You have my word. I won't hurt her. I promise."

Audrey sticks out her hand for me and I look at it in surprise, every instinct wanting me to take it and pull her into my arms, but I don't. Instead, I grasp her palm to mine, electricity tingling between us, and shake. For better or worse, we're doing this.

7. Audrey

I RUSH TOWARDS THE RESTAURANT AND GIVE THE DOORMAN A brief smile, but my mind is on what awaits me on the other side. I've spent the last three days just trying to survive by burying myself in work and research on blood cancer. I wanted to believe with everything in me that somehow my dad had got it wrong, that there are other options.

But if what he says is right, and I have no reason to believe otherwise, then in a few months I lose my father. The one man who has been my constant, my hero, and I can't accept it. The other reason I've been secluded like a Tibetan monk is this deal with Hudson and all the revelations from last weekend. I still can't get my head around what we did, although there has always been an element of inevitability about us. Like this was always going to come to a head in some way. I just never dreamed it would be by us ending up married and then keeping the ruse going for all the wrong reasons.

I haven't even wrapped my head around Tia and what it all means about the past we share.

Beck waves at me from a large table in the corner of the restaurant where all my friends are waiting for me. I wanted to tell them altogether, so I'd only have to explain it once, but now, as my stomach pitches, I wonder if I can bail without it seeming obvious that something is going on.

No. I have to do this and then I can answer any questions they have before I put it to bed.

"Hey, honey."

Lottie stands to kiss my cheek, as does Linc, who is sitting beside his wife. I sit between Lottie and Ryker, and he wraps an arm around my shoulders and kisses my head as his beautiful wife smiles at us. God, these two are so in love it's almost suffocating, but I'd never begrudge any of my friends what they've found. I love that they're all so in love. I just wish it didn't make me want the same thing when I know my life isn't on that path.

"Hey." I offer Lottie a smile that feels forced. "How is the mommy to be?"

"Good. The nausea comes and goes. I just need my husband to relax and understand I'm pregnant, not sick."

My glance slides to my cousin, who shrugs. He's super protective of Lottie and I know it's because he almost lost her through his own idiocy. Personally, I like seeing him this way. A man who isn't afraid to show the world how much he adores the woman he's with is refreshing. Although all my friends are the same. It's like being trapped in a romance book with all the alpha heroes.

"We ordered you an Old Fashioned."

Ryker pushes the glass toward me, and I take a grateful sip, letting the alcohol burn and warm me from the inside. I need this liquid courage right now, but it sits uncomfortably on my empty stomach. Eating hasn't been high on my list of priorities of late, and, honestly, my appetite has been virtually nothing.

I look around the table and see Beck with Amelia between him and Xander. Norrie is next to him, and then beside her, his arm around the back of her chair protectively, is Harrison. Eden and Ryker are heading off on their honeymoon tomorrow and I can see how perfect they are for each other with just one glance.

"So, are we doing this before or after we eat because I'm starving?"

"Beck, be patient."

He grasps the hand that Amelia has slapped across his chest and brings her fingertip to his lips with a sexy smile that's so intimate and tender it makes my chest ache.

"Let's get this over with now so I can relax."

I'm not sure I mean those words, but I want to. I blow out a breath and sit up taller, knowing that no matter what, my friends will have my back. They might not agree with anything I'm doing but they'll support me one hundred percent. To me, that is priceless.

"I'm not sure if Lincoln told you." I eye my cousin and he shakes his head no, although I know that doesn't include Lottie, as she was there when I broke the news to him. "My father is dying." Conversation breaks out across the table but my eyes are on Beck as I hold up my hand. "I need to get this out."

Everyone goes silent as Lottie reaches for my one hand and Ryker the other, and I take them, grateful for their support. "He has Myeloma and it's end stage."

I know by the look of regret that passes my friend's face that he recognizes the truth.

Lottie squeezes my hand harder as Ryker hugs me tight. "Oh, Audrey, I'm so sorry."

"Thank you."

"So, what is that?"

"Beck?"

I motion for him to explain because I need a second to gather myself and he'll give a clean, clinical explanation better than I ever could. He might be a heart surgeon, but he's a wonderful doctor and I know he did a rotation in oncology before he decided to specialize in cardiology. Sipping my drink, I wish I was anywhere but here having to give this news, but I'm not. Wishes are pointless. They never come true.

The Enemy

Once Beck has finished, I feel the eyes of all my friends on me and blink back tears.

"We're here for you, Audrey," Harrison says with sincerity.

"Please, don't be nice to me right now or I'm going to flood this place with tears."

"Okay. Subject change. What about your new husband?"

I glance at Ryker, grateful to him for changing the subject. "Hudson and I clearly overindulged at the wedding and ended up getting hitched."

"So, what's the plan? You getting it annulled?"

Xander is blunt and I like that about him. He's so perfect for Beck and Amelia, and I love the way they fit so seamlessly. I feel the blush stain my cheeks and hate that my complexion is so pale. "No, we're going to get a divorce, but not yet."

I'm hoping the second part of my sentence distracts from the first part but realize I'm wrong when Norrie smirks at me. Damn her for being so perceptive.

"Why not yet?" Harrison waves the server away before they can interrupt as he asks the question.

"My parents. My father especially was ecstatic to hear I'd gotten married and is convinced a husband would help me transition through losing him more easily. I haven't got the heart to tell him it's all a big lie."

Linc quirks a brow. "And Carmichael is going along with this?"

"He is."

"Why?"

I've wondered that myself a hundred times. Hudson is getting nothing out of this apart from weekly dates and me at his house for four days a week. It makes no sense because he didn't even demand sex, which I thought he might, and, honestly, I probably would've agreed. But he didn't.

"Honestly, I don't know. He said I could tell you guys the truth but that he wants the rest of the world to think this is real and that's what I need too if I want to sell this to my parents."

"This sounds suspicious to me."

I glance at Linc around Lottie and offer him a small smile. " I get it, I do. And I know you're trying to look out for the company, but he signed a contract this morning saying he won't touch Kennedy in the divorce. In fact, he wants nothing from me."

Lincoln's frown deepens. "I don't give a fuck about the company. I'm worried about you. He hurt you so badly, Audrey, and I don't want to see him do it again."

My heart seems to tighten in my chest at my cousin's fierce protectiveness and tears sting my eyes as I blink them back furiously. If I cry now, I won't stop for the rest of the day. I know because that was how I spent Monday after leaving Hudson in his office. "Thank you, but I won't let that happen. This is a business arrangement, that's all."

Lottie raised her hand as she grinned. "I speak from experience when I say that business arrangements between people who have history and sexual chemistry don't always end up how you expect."

"Hey." Linc tugs her closer to his side, his arms around her waist and Lottie tips her head to gift him with a loving look. "I didn't mean it ended in a bad way. I wouldn't change our story because it got us here, but all I'm saying is nothing is ever business when emotions are involved."

"Well, then, it will be fine because I have no emotions on this playing field." If I was in church, I would be in flames, for my blatant lie.

"So, you stay married until..." Ryker tails off, not wanting to say the words any more than I do.

"Yes."

"So, until then, we all act like you're the last of the deliriously happy couples amongst us?"

"Yes, please."

I hear a groan from beside me and see Linc bury his head in his wife's neck. "Do we have to?"

The Enemy

My lips itch in the first genuine smile I've felt in days. "Yes, you do. So be nice, or else."

Linc lifts his head and seems to have a silent conversation with his wife before he nods.

"Fine, I'll be good."

I envy the way they can do that. The connection they share is so intense and deep, it's like they're one person sometimes. That they found their way back to each other is a miracle to me, but then maybe fate is a thing. Linc fucked up so bad and yet Lottie forgave him. He even gave her the small wedding she wanted with just family and friends last month when he wanted the world and their dog to see them get hitched.

"Okay, now can we eat?"

I grin at Beck, who winks at me, and I love him for making this easier. I know I'll have a thousand questions to answer at some point but, for now, I can relax.

Lunch is louder than I expected and filled with everyone talking over each other, sharing news and tidbits of gossip. Banter is friendly and sometimes harsh but filled with love and, as I sit back and watch it, I know that I'll get through whatever life throws my way because I have these people with me every step.

It doesn't stop the loneliness from wrapping its arms around me though, and I'm reminded of the fact that when I go home tonight it will be to an empty house. Nobody to greet me and pour me a glass of wine or hold me in the dead of night when everything seems hopeless.

"Hey, you want to go shopping with us?"

Eden is leaning over Ryker and I snap out of my pity party. I have things to do, but right now I don't want to be alone with my thoughts because they either lead to my father and the huge overwhelming loss I face, or to Hudson and the confusion I feel over him. "Sure, sounds nice."

Beck grabs the check and I stand on the sidelines as all these alpha males kiss their wives like they might never see them again. I feel apart and yet included and, for a second, I wonder what it would be like if Hudson was here. Would he kiss me like the thought of a few hours apart was too much or would we be awkward and stilted? Because no matter how much my teenage self wants it, we aren't real, and I need to keep remembering that.

We step onto the street and my car slides up beside us, my driver, Nick, holding the door open as we all pile inside. One of the perks of my name is having a driver at my beck and call. Although I prefer to drive myself at weekends.

"We're going shopping, Nick, so you know what that means?"

Nick is a fifty-year-old father of four daughters and, although they don't shop in the same stores as I do, he knows where I want to go.

He grins and tips his head. "Sure thing, Miss Kennedy."

"That's Mrs. Carmichael," Amelia pipes up from beside me.

I freeze at the name. I know the media has been banding it around like a hooker at a bachelor party, but it is the first time I am hearing it.

"Oops. Sorry, Mrs. Carmichael."

"Amelia!"

"What it's true. You are Mrs. Carmichael."

"I know but...."

But what? Why do I mind so much? Probably because I spent so long wishing it was my name and now hearing it throws me for a loop.

"But nothing."

I shut the barrier between Nick and myself so I could talk freely to my friends. I close my eyes and rub the sides of my temples where a headache is forming. When I open my eyes, I find four sets of eyes watching me with varying degrees of question in them.

"What?"

"Well, was the sex good?"

"Norrie?" I stammer at her brazen question.

"What? That man has some serious Big Dick Energy."

"He really does."

Eden nods and I scowl, making her wince. I feel bad for a second because she's the newest to our group of friends and I know I can seem a little fierce sometimes. "Sorry." I pat her knee and her smile returns.

"It's fine. This must be a lot to take in."

"You have no idea. I have to live with him four days a week and somehow find the energy to do my job, exercise, spend as much precious time with my dad as I can, and learn how to interact with a ten-year-old girl. And, on top of that, I have to try not to fall at my new husband's feet and beg him to fuck me until none of it matters."

I pause and glance up to see open-mouthed faces watching me.

"What?" I whisper yell at them and the slack jaws morph as each of them cracks up laughing. I'm speechless until suddenly I'm laughing too. Tears are pouring down my face until I'm hiccupping with it.

"Oh, my goodness. Do you feel better now you got that out of your system?"

"No." I wipe tears from my cheeks. "I feel fucking horny."

"So, call your handsome husband to come fuck you dirty."

I shake my head. "No, I told him if he brought his dick near me I'd bite it off."

"Ouch."

"I know, although he did offer to take care of my needs because, in his words, he doesn't share and the only place his dick will be is either in my pussy or my mouth."

Norrie fans her face dramatically. "That's hot."

I nod. "It is, and I hate that I want him so much."

Amelia cocks her head. "What happened between you two?"

Lottie throws up her hands. "Are we just not addressing the comment about a ten-year-old child? He has a kid?"

I groan, not sure if I can share all of it, but I want to share some of it. I'm sick of carrying this burden alone. I never had a girl squad before, not one I could trust with my deepest secrets. Now I do, I want to share with them like they have with me. Linc is great, as are the boys, but girlfriends give you a very different perspective. "I'm gonna need cocktails after shopping and then I'll share all the details, I promise. But I will say this, Tia is his sister, not his daughter."

Lottie cocks her head but says no more and I'm grateful. I need a little time to get what I want to share straight in my head. Lucky for me, Norrie is here to lighten the tension.

"Oh yeah, momma's getting some monkey sex tonight."

My eyes widen at Norrie and then we all burst out laughing.

8. Audrey

SHOPPING WITH FRIENDS IS MUCH MORE FUN THAN SHOPPING alone or with a personal shopper. We spent over an hour trying to convince Eden that she needed to buy five new swimsuits for her honeymoon when we all know Ryker is going to keep her naked ninety percent of the time anyway.

"Are we ready for cocktails now?" Amelia asks with a wink.

"God, yes. My feet are killing me," Norrie moans, glaring at me in my four-inch pumps.

"What? I can't help it I can rock these babies without crying like a baby."

Norrie gives me a rude gesture as I wrap my arm around her neck and kiss her cheek. Champagne, and apple juice for Lottie and Eden, flowed as we shopped, each sales assistant hoping that booze and flattery would make us spend more.

"You love me really."

"I do, but only because you're going to spill your guts about the hunky Hudson."

"You remembered that, huh?"

"Yes," they chorus as we step into the reception of the luxury Bellman Hotel. Heads turn to look at us, a sneer of distaste on their faces ready to reprimand anyone who dares to interrupt their quiet, but the snooty assholes soon smile when they realize who we are.

God, I hate people.

"Miss Kennedy, it's a pleasure to see you again. Can I get you a table in the lounge?"

The hostess is eyeing us as if we've stolen her favorite toys from the sale, and she hates that she has to be nice. I almost feel sorry for her. Four of the most eligible bachelors in the country are married to my friends and I have the pleasure of bursting another bubble.

"That's Mrs. Carmichael, actually."

Her cheeks go red, and she nods. "Apologies, I wasn't... I didn't...." I widen my eyes as she stutters. "Follow me."

The hostess scurries off and I watch Eden roll her lips between her teeth.

We're seated in a private corner reserved for the wealthiest and most important guests.

"Is this table okay, Mrs. Carmichael?"

"Yes, thank you."

The stunning redhead nods and hands us cocktail menus. "A server will be over shortly to take your order."

I can see that being nice to us is like sucking on a lemon and it makes me enjoy it more. I know women like her, they're vultures. Every time I go out with Beck, Ryker, Lincoln, and Harrison women like her paw at them and make it clear that they'll happily drop their panties for a quick fuck and the chance to say they screwed one of the Kings of Ruin.

"Audrey, that was mean."

I wave a hand. "Oh, please. That woman has fucked more married men than I've had glasses of champagne."

Eden pales.

"Don't worry, none of your husbands would be stupid enough to go there."

The Enemy

A server sidles up to us and she looks professional and friendly without being too friendly. "What can I get you ladies?"

We all order our cocktails or mocktails and wait until we're alone before the talk turns to Hudson again. I pick at the breadsticks on the table, my appetite isn't great right now but I hardly touched breakfast and if I don't eat something, I'll be passed out before happy hour.

"Well?"

"Well, what?"

I point a breadstick at Amelia who was brave enough to ask and she breaks the end off and steals half.

"Hudson. What happened between you two? You're like feral beasts around each other half the time."

As I'm about to answer, I see Lottie look over my shoulder, her eyes widening. "Oh, shit."

"What?" I turn, my heart in my throat, and see Hudson walk in with Felicity Marchand, the famous supermodel. I feel the hair on my neck go up as I look at them together and something hot and dangerous bubbles in my blood. I want to study them objectively, him tall, dark, and handsome with a dangerous air about him that calls to me. Her tall, blonde, with striking blue eyes and a figure to die for. He bends to listen to something she's saying and laughs, and I see red.

"Audrey, no."

I ignore Amelia's warning and stride toward my husband in name only, with no idea of what I want to say to him when I get there. His head comes up and I see shock on his face. Ha! Serves that cheating rat bastard right, but then his face morphs into a show-stopping smile that makes me want to drop to my knees. My steps falter but he's already walking toward me.

"Darling, I didn't know you would be here today."

I still as he takes me in his arms, his hand low on my back, almost caressing the top of my ass, his palm on the side of my neck. His smile is wide and open and, if I didn't know the truth, I'd see a man who was delighted to see his wife.

"It wasn't planned."

"Well, it's a pleasant surprise for me."

He dips his head and I go to turn my head, but his fingers capture my jaw and hold me in his firm grip. I think he'll drop a perfunctory kiss on my lips to seal our story, but he doesn't. Hudson kisses me like he hasn't breathed air in years and I'm his only source.

Firm lips slant over mine as he pushes his tongue in to tease against mine. I sigh against him as he brings his hand up, cupping my head, his hard body pressing against me. And I mean hard, his dick is like a giant stick of rock against my lower belly, and it makes me want to rub against him like a cat and purr.

He pulls away and pins me with his intense gaze, his dark eyes latent with hunger. "Missed you."

Those two words pack such a punch I can't speak because they're laced with so much sincerity, that for a second only we exist.

"Wow, that was hot."

We both startle like we'd forgotten everyone else was there and, for a moment, I'd done just that. He consumes me, he always has. I step back and he lets me go, but not far, his hand sliding into my palm and that sweet contact affects me as much as the kiss did.

Norrie is munching on a breadstick as she watches us from just beside me. Lottie, Amelia, and Eden are standing with her like my emotional support team.

"Hey, Hudson."

"Ladies, it's a pleasure to see you again. I see you're keeping my wife entertained."

I want to glare at him, but we have every eye in the room on us and it causes nerves to take flight in my belly. I'm used to being looked at because of who I am but the role I've molded into my own personal shield won't work here. I have to play the devoted wife. As if sensing my nerves, Hudson glances at me, giving me a wink that makes my knees weak as his thumb strokes over my palm in a soothing motion.

Fuck, why does he have to be so hot and sweet? I'm starting to think this might have been a mistake.

The Enemy

"Not as entertained as you just made her." I elbow Amelia in the ribs, and she winces and glares at me. "Oi."

"Darling, I want you to meet Felicity Marchand. She's a client of mine."

I can practically feel my lip curling in a snarl as I look at the supermodel every man on the planet wants to bang. "Felicity, it's very nice to meet you."

I hold out my hand to be polite and she takes it with a genuine smile that I wasn't expecting.

"Lovely to meet you, too." She turns to Hudson as I drop her hand and lifts her brows. "She's out of your weight class, Hudson."

I still at her words but Hudson squeezes my hand gently as he throws his head back and laughs and it's beautiful. He's always been beautiful, and that's what makes him so dangerous to me.

"She's out of my league in every way you can imagine, Felicity, and, believe me, I know it."

Something about those words makes me frown. Reminding me of the times when we were young and he'd vow to make himself worthy of me. My stomach tightens in a knot and I cock my head to see him watching me. "He's not out of anyone's league. He never has been."

A small smile ghosts his lips before he turns away and I hate that I miss his eyes on me. He bends to kiss my cheek and I fight the urge to turn into his kiss as his lips press against my skin.

"I'll let you get back to your friends. I'll see you later."

I nod and spin. As I make my way back to our table, my friends are on my heels. Deliberately, I sit with my back to Hudson and Felicity, not wanting to see how good they look together or let him think I care.

Amelia wiggles her eyebrows as she sucks her Mojito through a straw. "So, fess up. What happened between you two? Because whatever it is, it didn't kill the insane chemistry you have. And I should know. I am a scientist, after all."

Eden throws a napkin at Amelia. "Alright nerd, no need to make the rest of us feel stupid."

"Ha, speak for yourself. I got my son sleeping through the night. I feel like a damn genius." Norrie fist bumps the air as Lottie lifts her hand for a high-five.

This is why I love these women, we're all so different and we celebrate each other for that.

"Fine, whatever. You don't need a degree to see that Audrey and her handsome husband have some serious heat."

"I thought I might need a minute alone with my bullet after that kiss." Eden sips her drink with a smile.

"Right, it was hot. So come on, out with it. Give us something."

"Fine. Hudson and I were together in college. I thought it was perfect, he was perfect, but then he ghosted me."

Four pairs of eyes are staring at me.

"And?" Amelia asks, rolling her hand for more.

I throw my hands up. "And what? That's it."

Norrie leans back and shakes her head. "Bullshit. You don't hold a grudge like you have because you got ghosted."

My skin prickles as I feel his gaze on me, and I refuse to turn around and give him the satisfaction of thinking I care.

"Maybe Hudson will tell us what happened."

Norrie pushes her chair back and I panic, standing to stop her. She may be small but she's mighty and, surviving what she has, I'm glad for it. But right now, I want to lock her in a box and dump her in the ocean.

"Okay, fine. Stop. I'll tell you."

"No more holding out on us. We're your friends and we love you."

A lump lodges in my throat and I nod. "I know and I love you guys, too. I just don't find this kind of thing easy."

Lottie reaches over and grips my hand.

"I met Hudson in my first lecture. We were both doing business, but for me, it was my main degree and for him, it was a module of his law degree. He was..." I look up as memories flood me of the boy who stole my heart with his crooked smile. "He was everything. You've seen him, so you know how gorgeous he is. Back then, it was tempered with a cute shyness. He rode this death trap of a motorbike and, unlike the others, I knew his focus wasn't on getting drunk. It was on his education."

"Cute, hot nerd with a motorbike, I like it. Go on." Norrie nods with a grin.

"We got together pretty quickly but it was always in our little bubble. He got on okay with the guys, but I always got the feeling he preferred it when it was just us. Not in a bad way. I think he just felt uncomfortable around them. Hudson was on a scholarship, and I think our wealth was a turn-off for him. Ironically, it was one of the things I loved about him. He didn't care that I had money or a trust fund, and he'd always insist on paying when we went out. He made me feel like he wanted me for me."

"Swoon." Eden sighs as she listens, her chin in her palms.

"We fell in love, and I thought he was the one. Then one night, he just disappeared without a word. We'd just... you know."

"Fucked like bunnies?" Amelia asks.

I laugh and shake my head. "No, it was always more than that with us. I went to the bathroom and, when I came out, he was gone. I didn't think anything of it but when he didn't call or answer his door in the dorms, I started to worry. He didn't talk about his family much, but I knew it was just him and his mom. I went to see him and when I did, my heart shattered."

Just the memory of that night still has the ability to shred my heart into ribbons. I know in my heart I should explain all of the situation, but I just don't have it in me to do so without falling apart and my grasp on my emotions is too tenuous right now to try. "He was walking towards his apartment with a tiny baby in his arm, and his other arm around a woman. He looked at her with so much love and my heart broke. He'd kept this whole other life from me and shattered everything we had into a web of lies, or so I thought."

Pulling my Old Fashioned towards me, I take a huge sip and then look up at my friends. Lottie looks like she wants to go over to Hudson and string him up by his balls, her angry gaze aimed behind me. But I can't let her because somehow in this mess, I got it wrong. Tia was the baby I saw that day and I have to find a way to talk to him about it and clear the air if we have any hope of pulling this ruse off.

"His sister?" Lottie murmurs, understanding immediately.

"What a dick!" Eden wrinkles her nose as she raises her hand to indicate we want another round of drinks.

"You want me to have Xander kick his ass?" Amelia offers with a quirk of her lips.

I know she's joking but if I wanted her to do it, I know she would and that thought gives me the courage I need to finish this story and admit my mistake. "Yes, his much younger sister. Turns out that Tia," I smile just thinking of the adorable little girl. "That's her name. Well, she's the baby I saw and the woman I must have seen with him was his mother."

Norrie sits back stunned. "Oh, wow."

"I know, right. It's insane. I spent all this time thinking he cheated on me and had a child behind my back, when, in fact, she's his sister."

"But why ghost you? Why not just tell you?"

I glance at Amelia and shrug. "I don't know. I know his mom died when Tia was a baby, but now the circumstances and Tia is..." I don't want to explain this in a way that makes Tia sound like anything but the beautiful gift I know she is to Hudson. Watching him with her, I can see she's the light of his life, but it had to have been tough for him. "Tia has Downs Syndrome and I suspect it has been anything but easy for him. He's also ridiculously protective of her."

I look for any sign of judgment in my friends' faces and find none, which doesn't surprise me.

"Hudson never talked about his mom being pregnant?"

"No, he was always very tight-lipped about her, and I never pushed it."

The Enemy

Lottie offers me a kind smile. "You should talk to him. Clear the air a bit. I don't pretend to be the expert but whatever is between you two isn't finished. That much I do know."

I see her look behind me as she speaks, and I feel him before I even turn. Somehow, when Hudson is near, all the oxygen in the room seems to thin until I can hardly catch my breath.

A gentle hand lands on my waist and it takes everything in me not to lean into his touch.

"Hey."

I angle my head up to look at him and damn near stop breathing from the look of heat in his eyes. "Hi."

"I'm cooking Thursday night and wanted to check if you still like lasagna?"

I nod and clear my throat. "Yes, love it."

His smile widens. "Great. It's Tia's favorite."

"Perfect."

We share a look, and I don't even know what it means, but it's soft as if a truce has been called between us and I need that right now. I don't have enough ball-busting energy right now to fake it with him. And honestly, I miss him and the friendship we had, as well as all the other things we shared.

"I'll see you Thursday night."

I nod and he drops a kiss on my shoulder, which shouldn't make my knees weak, but that simple touch is so intimate, that my belly flips over, igniting a heat inside me that threatens to burn me from the inside out. "See you then."

I congratulate myself on getting the words out without a single sign of my inner turmoil showing but he notices the slightly breathless way it comes out and winks before giving my waist a squeeze and striding away.

I follow the confident, almost arrogant, way he prowls toward the exit, trying not to notice how his suit pants hug his ass, but it's so hard when I know what he looks like naked.

God, why can't I remember anything from Saturday night? What a waste.

"Yep, definitely not over between you two."

I don't acknowledge Amelia's comment because there's little point in denying what's plain to see. There's still something there. I just hope whatever it is, it doesn't burn us both to cinders.

9. Hudson

"How long now, Huddy?"

I'm grating the cheese for the top of the lasagna when Tia asks how long before Audrey arrives, for what feels like the hundredth time in ten minutes. It's cute how excited she is to see her, but it does nothing to ease the nerves I feel. I've wrestled with my decision to let Audrey into my sister's life since I agreed to it. I don't want my baby sister hurt. But, equally, I'm selfish when it comes to Audrey and want her to see this part of my life, to be involved in this part of my life, even if I only get her for a short time. "Not long now."

As I finish the words, I get an alert on my phone to say the gate has been accessed. She's here and suddenly it's not Tia who's excited, it's me. Seeing her on Tuesday had been a surprise but being allowed to touch her in public in the way I've craved to do for so long was fucking perfect.

Seeing the look of jealousy on her face as she strode towards Felicity and I had made me so hard it took everything in me not to drag her to the nearest closet and kiss her until she admitted she wanted me too. Taking her in my arms and kissing her, touching her had been as natural as breathing to me. It was what I've wanted for so long. The ease with which I fell back into that head space, it felt like no time had passed between us.

We were, in some ways, those same kids madly in love with each other, and nothing and nobody mattered when we were together. Except everything is different now. We aren't those kids, and she isn't in love with me like I am with her. She wants me, I know that, but she's holding on to the hurt I caused her. A hard shell has formed around her that I helped build and she isn't the same girl I loved. But neither am I the poor boy with holes in his clothes living on noodles.

Now I charge five figures for an hour of my time and will never spend my fortune in a lifetime if I tried. I'll never be as rich as Audrey, nor will I ever have the pedigree of Beck or Lincoln, but I'm a man I'm proud to look at in the mirror each morning. My only regret in life is the one who's just pulled up in front of my house.

"She's here."

Wiping my hands on a cloth slung over my shoulder, I round the island and follow the sound of Tia's infectious excitement. She looks ready to burst as she waits by the door for me to answer it. She knows better than to answer the door.

"Hurry, Huddy."

"Alright, kid. I'm coming."

I grip the handle and pull open the door and there she is, the woman who has both me and my sister hanging onto her every word. Her hair is down in thick dark waves around her shoulders, and she's wearing a cream cashmere sweater under a black leather biker jacket. Wide-leg jeans do nothing to hide her incredible figure before her long legs end in spiked black heels that make me want to drop to my knees.

"Belle." Tia squeals and launches herself at Audrey, her thin arms going around Audrey's tiny waist.

I freeze for a second wondering what Audrey will do and desperate for her not to reject my sister.

"Hey, gorgeous girl. It's good to see you, too."

The Enemy

As Audrey wraps Tia in a warm hug, I feel my shoulders relax and a smile overtakes my face. "Let Audrey through the door, Tia."

I step back as Audrey looks up and offers me a small smile filled with nerves. God, she's beautiful. Even with the slightly dark circles under her eyes and the exhaustion that I can feel clinging to her, she's stunning.

"Something smells good."

I take the bag she's carrying from her hands as I lead the way into the combined kitchen dining room. "It won't be long. Do you want to see your room first?"

Tia cocks her head at me. "But, Huddy, Audrey is in your room. Elliot at school told me married people sleep together."

Audrey coughs through a laugh as both the women in my life regard me. I scratch my chin to buy myself a second to get out of this. "Well, that's true. But you see, the thing is, Audrey snores really bad."

An outraged gasp escapes her. "I do not."

Tia leans into Audrey and I love the natural way my wife embraces my sister.

"See, she doesn't so she can sleep with you."

Audrey's mouth opens and closes as she realizes she just fell into her own trap. I smirk as she scowls at me, and I feel contented happiness sweep through me. "I guess she can."

"Can we play dolls after dinner?"

I go to answer as I check the timer on the oven, but Tia isn't asking me, she's gazing longingly at Audrey. I get it. Boy, do I get it. I feel the same look on my face when I look at her too.

Audrey looks to me for help and I nod. "Sure, but only if Audrey doesn't mind and only if your homework is done."

"Yay."

Tia runs off, most likely to bring every doll she owns down into the lounge, and I'm left alone for the first time with the woman who owns my heart. My every instinct wants me to take her in my arms and erase every ounce of the exhaustion I see on her face, but I know

I have to take this slow and not overwhelm her. "Would you like a glass of wine?"

"Yes, that would be lovely."

She wipes her palm down her thigh, and I want to reassure her, but she turns her head away, moving as she takes in my space. I busy myself, pouring her a glass of her favorite white wine.

"I can give you the tour after dinner." As I hand her the glass, our fingers brush, and that pull that's always there when she's near dances over my fingertips.

"Thank you. That would be nice."

I lean against the island, marveling at the fact she is in my home.

"Aren't you going to have a glass?"

I shake my head. "Not tonight. Tia has a bit of a cold, so I want to make sure I'm totally fine to drive unimpaired just in case."

Audrey stops with the glass halfway to her luscious lips. "Is that likely? Is she okay?"

I offer her a grin as the timer goes off on the oven. I grab the oven glove and pull the still bubbling lasagna from the oven, placing it on a trivet to cool, while I dress a salad. It also gives me a chance to collect my thoughts.

"Tia had a few health issues when she was younger. Her heart mainly and it makes a simple cold take on a very different possibility for her. She's mostly well. I just have to be vigilant."

"Oh, I didn't know." Audrey shakes her head, placing the glass of wine on the side as if she lost her taste for it suddenly.

I hate that I've landed that weight on her delicate shoulders. "How could you?"

She looks up, her eyebrow arched. "Indeed."

I chuckle at her statement, the slight dig about the secret I kept well-earned. "I deserve that."

Audrey sighs. "No, you didn't. I shouldn't have said it."

"You can ask me anything, Audrey, and I'll answer you honestly. You have my word."

She purses her lips as if thinking and then gives her head a tiny shake. "Let's just have a nice dinner. I have dolls to play with and I think I might need all my mental fortitude for that."

"Oh, you definitely will. Tia will have you playing all night. Believe me, I know."

"You're good with her."

I glance at Tia as she walks back into the kitchen with her favorite doll under her arm and can't help the wave of love I feel for her. "She makes it easy."

Dinner is a relaxed, lively affair and I barely get a word in as Tia and Audrey chat away like they've known each other for years. I hadn't really considered how the lack of a female figure, like Audrey, would affect Tia. While we have Mrs. Price, she's older and struggles to do certain things. Tia is basking in Audrey's infectious light and it's crystal clear that Audrey feels the same.

Seeing this warm, gentle side of Audrey after feeling her hatred for so long, makes me desperately want to do the one thing I know I never can; turn back the clock. After dinner, I'm banished to the kitchen so that the girls can play. I can't say I'm mad about it, not when it allows me the privilege of hearing so much laughter and joy coming from the den.

Standing with my shoulder against the door jamb, I cross my arms and watch Tia and Audrey together, and a longing for something so far out of reach it's almost impossible hits me. This. I want this to be what I come home to every night. The two people who own different parts of my heart together making memories.

Audrey looks up as she cradles a doll in her arms and our eyes lock. So much is still unsaid, so much raw emotion still standing between us, but for the first time in a long time, I have hope that maybe one day I could have the unthinkable.

"Huddy, are you playing?"

Pushing off the door, I walk into the den and crouch beside Audrey, her scent light and sweet and oh so familiar.

"How about we give Audrey a tour of the house? We don't want her getting lost in the middle of the night and walking into the window."

Tia giggles. "Huddy, you're so silly."

"What!" I yell in fake outrage as I grab my sister and toss her over my shoulder, running around the room with her.

"Belle, help me. A monster has me."

"I'll save you from the beast, Tia."

Audrey jumps up and gives chase as I roar. "I'm the beast, and I'll lock you in my tower."

Audrey's arms come around me as she tries to stop me, and I go to my knees as I let the girls tackle me into submission. Tia jumps on my chest as I slump to my back, and Audrey grabs my arms and pulls them above my head as she kneels by my head.

"Tickle him, Tia."

I arch my brow at Audrey. Her knowledge of my hatred for tickling not playing in my favor.

"Tia, don't you dare."

There's zero threat in my voice, and I know Tia is having the time of her life.

Audrey looks at Tia and nods. "Do it."

"Ms. Kennedy, you're going to pay for that."

Audrey arches a brow and smirks. "It's Mrs. Carmichael, actually."

A growl of satisfaction rolls up my throat at the sound of her calling herself my wife. God, what I wouldn't give for it to be real. To be able to take her in my arms and kiss her until neither of us can catch our breath.

Tia pounces on me and we wrestle as she tries to tickle me, and Audrey holds me down because I let her. When Tia starts to cough from over-exertion, I relent and help her sit up, pulling her onto my lap.

"Steady on, kiddo." I rub her little back as Audrey watches on with a worried look.

Tia begins to settle, and I catch Audrey's concerned gaze. "She's fine. Just a little winded from trying to tickle me when she has a cold. Time to settle down, munchkin."

"But, Huddy."

I shake my head. "No arguments. You know the rules." Tia knows this tone of voice means not to bother arguing so she doesn't. "How about I read you two stories instead of one to make up for the early night?"

"I want Audrey to do it."

I glance at Audrey and shake my head. "Why don't we let Audrey settle down and explore her new home?"

"No, it's fine. I'd love to read her stories. If you don't mind, that is?"

I shake my head as I realize just how easy it's going to be for me to fall headfirst into this fake relationship and never want to come back out.

10. Audrey

"And they all lived happily ever after."

I look down at the sleeping child who is snuggled against my side and can't help the compulsion to lean in and kiss her strawberry-scented head. Hudson had turned on some kind of vapor machine that was filling the room with the light scent of eucalyptus. He said it helped with her congestion and actually it's almost pleasant.

"She's out."

I look and find Hudson watching us with a soft look on his face. To say that tonight wasn't what I expected would be a lie. Although, if I'm honest, I'm not really sure what I was expecting. But it wasn't something so domesticated. When I usually see him, he's dressed in a tailored three-piece suit and looks every inch the cunning, cut-throat lawyer he is in the courtroom. Here he's just Huddy, who cooks and cleans up after dinner and then plays dolls or reads with his sister because it makes her smile.

Hudson steps forward as I move to extract myself from Tia without disturbing her. He kneels beside her bed and tucks her in tight, dropping a kiss on her head, and I get a pang of longing in my belly. This was what I imagined all those years ago when we were together. This simple life, only the child would have been ours. Not that I don't love how he stepped up for his sister, but then, that's who Hudson is. It's who he's always been.

Our complex history and the betrayal I imagined make it hard to remember the boy I fell in love with, but it's coming back hard and fast now.

I wait, watching as Hudson turns on the night light beside her bed and moves to the door quietly, and pulls it almost closed. Following him down the stairs, I glance at the door I know is his room across the hallway and then the one further down, which is one of the spare rooms.

His room had been exactly what I expected. Dark wood armoire, thick cream carpet, king-size bed, and a view out over the front of the house. A bathroom off the bedroom holds a bath and shower, and I am dying to sink into a bath and let all the tension from the last few days drain away. I'm not sure if it will work but already, I feel the burden of everything I carry easing.

Perhaps it's this familial bubble I find myself in or maybe it's being around Hudson again. He always had the ability to chase away the stress of my life.

As we enter the kitchen, he holds up the bottle of wine. "Another glass?"

I shake my head as I twist my fingers with nerves. Why am I suddenly nervous without Tia as a buffer between us? "No, thank you."

Hudson cocks his head. "You don't have to feel bad for indulging when I'm not. Honestly, I'm most likely overreacting about Tia. It's just a cold but I'm a bit over-protective when it comes to her."

He rubs the back of his neck as if he's slightly embarrassed and his t-shirt rides up, exposing a sliver of tanned abs, which do nothing to stop the riot of butterflies in my belly from taking flight. Ever since he rushed out of the bathroom at our hotel last weekend in nothing but bubbles, I've been fantasizing about his cut body. Thick, muscular thighs, six-pack abs, with a slight sprinkle of hair, sculpted pectorals, and wide shoulders. Even his throat is sexy, with a defined Adam's apple, that I want to run my tongue down.

"No, honestly, I have a meeting with my new board for the media section of Kennedy tomorrow, so I need a clear head." I expect him to ask me about it. Most men find the fact I'm CFO of such a huge legacy company before I hit thirty so astounding that it's all they want to know about.

"How about a chamomile tea, instead? Do you still like tea?"

A smile crawls over my lips at his question and the fact he remembers such an insignificant thing and I voice it. "I can't believe you remember that."

Hudson turns back from where he is filling water into a kettle and gives me a flirty grin. "I remember everything when it comes to you, Belle."

God, this man will be the death of me. He has my emotions running around like a headless chicken. Part of me is holding on to that well-established resentment out of habit, and the rest of me is fluctuating between being so horny I want to climb him like a tree and remembering everything we shared and sinking into that soft cloud of teenage love.

Pulling up a stool at the island, I watch him move around the kitchen with practiced ease, his movements controlled and light. "Will Tia sleep through now or will she wake?"

"She'll sleep most likely. She's always slept well unless she's sick, and then it's rough. A cold shouldn't stop her, but I'll check in on her before I go to bed. You can take my room and I'll take the guest room next to hers."

I want to argue that I will take the guest room, but a part of me wants to be in his space and I don't want to rock this fragile peace we have established tonight.

He hands me a mug with a princess on the side and I lift my eyebrow as he smirks.

"Seemed appropriate."

"I don't see you holding a beast mug."

The Enemy

Hudson holds a hand over his chest as he rocks back pretending to look wounded. "I'm Prince Charming."

"I prefer the beast."

His gaze flies to mine and the heat and sexual tension pulls tight between us. Chemistry has never been our problem. No, our problem was always communication. I need to change the subject and distract him from my stupid loaded comment.

"Is that why you never told anyone about Tia? Because you're protecting her?"

I wonder for a second if he'll allow me to get away with the change in direction before he seems to make a decision. Moving around the island, he takes the stool beside me and I angle my body so we face each other. It's intimate, the gap between us so small that if I turn slightly my knee will brush his thigh.

"It's not that I'm trying to hide Tia. I just don't tell people our business or talk about my home life at all. Who I am here in my home, isn't who I am to the world. I prefer this me, where I can be authentic, and only Tia and very few people get that."

"Surely some people know though. It's hard to keep a secret like a child."

He nods, scratching his chin. "Yes, some people know, but they've signed a watertight NDA contract."

"I haven't and neither have my friends."

Hudson's shoulders tense for just a second, before he lets it go with a breath. "I know. But rightly or wrongly, I trust you not to betray that. Tia means the world to me. She has since the nurse laid her in my arms the day she was born."

It's hard not to think of that time and not let the grief and pain overtake me, but that has no bearing on this conversation, so I just nod. "I like this side of you."

"Yeah, what else do you like?"

I know what he wants but if I go down this road with him, I'm not sure I'll ever find a way back. "Lines with less cheese in them."

Hudson throws his head back and laughs, and I can't help but join in, his genuine joy infectious. It strikes me that I've laughed more in this house in a few hours than I have for the last year. That's not to say I haven't been happy, but I haven't felt free. Which, considering the shit storm that is my life, is a miracle.

"Everything is better with cheese, Aud."

"Except pick-up lines."

Hudson holds his hand up with a grin. "Fair point."

We fall into a comfortable silence until he lifts his gaze from his mug and his expression is sobering. "I really am sorry about your dad, Aud."

My nose prickles with the familiar sting of emotion, but I refuse to cry again today. "Thank you."

"What do you need from me to make this easier on you and your parents?"

I'm surprised by the thoughtfulness of his question, but perhaps I shouldn't be. He was always this way when we dated too. I've just spent so long hating him that it's hard to turn off. We should clear the air and discuss what happened, but I don't want to fracture this truce we have right now or open myself up to questions I'm not ready to give him the answers to.

"Just pretend you're madly in love with me and ease their worries."

"Easy. What else?"

I shrug. "That's it I guess. Maybe be available for some family stuff. My parents will want to get to know you, especially my dad before he...." I can't finish the sentence and he doesn't make me, taking my hand and threading his fingers through mine.

"Look at me, Audrey."

My head tilts up and I find him watching me with undisguised emotion on his face that I can't place.

"I'm there whenever you need me to be. If you need us to spend every day visiting your dad, then that's what we do. Take it from me, losing a parent is hard so make those memories and have the conversations while you can."

The Enemy

My throat closes and I roll my lips between my teeth to try and fight those damn tears. "Thank you."

"I mean it. Anything you need, I'm here for you."

"What about Tia? I don't want to pull all your focus away from her. She needs you too."

"We'll make it work, okay?"

I haven't got it in me to argue and, honestly, the thought of having him to lean on feels good. I know I have my friends, but they all have their own lives, and I know I'll be filled with guilt for dragging them away from their partners. Hudson is offering and selfishly I'm going to take him up on this. "Okay."

"You wanna watch some TV?"

"No, I think I'll head to bed."

"Yeah, me too. It's been a long day."

I help him rinse the mugs and load the dishwasher, adding detergent as he gives the kitchen a final wipe-down. It's so normal and I find it soothing.

As we head up, I stop on the threshold of his bedroom and watch as he checks on Tia, peeking my head around the door to watch the silent interaction. He pulls the covers higher over her shoulders and gently presses the back of his hand to her forehead before retreating.

"She okay?"

"Yeah, she's fine. She'll be out 'til morning now, but if she comes in looking for me, just come get me."

I glance at my door and then back to Hudson, wondering if this is a really stupid idea.

"You know your bed is huge. We can share without it getting weird."

Hudson moves in closer to me until we're standing just inches away from each other. I'm not a short woman, but he still makes me feel tiny as he looms over me. My breath stalls in my chest as he dips his head so his lips are almost touching mine. I swear I might pass out from lack of oxygen as I fight the internal battle of whether I want him to kiss me or not. No, not a battle. I do want it, I just don't know if it's a good idea. If I could just access those memories, it might be easier.

"Audrey, if you want me in your bed, you're gonna have to ask, nicely."

My eyes narrow at the gravelly, deep statement and it takes my brain a second to catch up. I fold my arms indignantly as I step back and give him a glare that would fell most men. It doesn't even cause a flicker of a reaction and, God, I like that too. I don't want a man I can intimidate or push around. I want a man who can keep up with me, who can challenge me one minute and hold me in his arms and protect me the next. Urgh, I want Hudson, and I'll cut off my own arm before I admit it.

"Never gonna happen. I was trying to be nice, but I'd rather share a bed with a rabid dog than you."

To my irritation, Hudson's lips twitch in a smile as he steps back with a wink. "You know where I am if you change your mind."

Spinning on my heel, I head into his room to escape, closing the door silently so as not to disturb Tia and lean against the back.

Taking a quick shower, I change into satin, short pajamas and slide between the cool sheets of Hudson's bed. My skin feels sensitive as I lie down and the scent of him consumes my every pore. I can almost taste his skin on my tongue as I toss and turn. My body growing more and more aroused with every movement. He's everywhere in this room, and I can't help but imagine what it would be like to wake up wrapped in his arms. To roll over in the night and have him pull me to his side, even in sleep. To have his hands on me, in that space between sleep and awake where everything feels lazy and leisurely. Would he slide his hand between my legs? Would he kiss me and whisper all the dirty things he wanted to do? Or would he push his huge cock inside me, while I was barely awake, and fuck me into wakefulness with an earth-shattering orgasm?

The Enemy

I FALL INTO A FITFUL SLEEP FILLED WITH EROTIC IMAGES OF THE man across the hall from me and wake feeling groggy. I throw the covers off me when my alarm goes off and jump in the shower, determined to keep my head on straight for this meeting later today.

Dressing in a navy fitted dress with cap sleeves and a modest square neckline, I add a red belt and red heels to give it some color. I know I have to dress the part in my world, but I refuse to give in to the temptation to dress like I want to merge into the gray suit brigade. As a woman in business, I want to celebrate that, and dressing with my own signature gives me that little victory. I curl my dark hair into a low chignon and finish my make-up with a red lip, which screams 'I mean business'.

When I make it to the kitchen, I stop short when I see Hudson and Tia talking to an older woman. All eyes come to me so I force a smile and lift my head high.

"Good morning, Tia. Did you sleep well?" I move to her on instinct and place my hand on her back as she wraps an arm around my waist.

"Yes, but Huddy says I need to stay home today because of my cold."

I look to Hudson who is watching us closely. His clean-shaven jaw is half hidden by a mug of coffee. He has on a white shirt, navy suit pants, and a navy vest with a red tie, and anyone who didn't know would think we'd coordinated our looks. He looks delicious and all those images that kept me up last night blast back into my head.

"Well, he knows best."

"I guess."

I hate the dejected sound of her voice, and something in me wants to fix everything for this child. "How about I stop on my way home and get some new crafting stuff for us to do later?"

My eyes are on Hudson, but my question is for Tia. I see him give me a small nod, his eyes warm and it makes me stand taller.

"Yes. Can we make jewelry?"

"Of course. I'll get everything we need."

"What do you say, Tia?"

I glance at Mrs. Price, who Hudson explained helps him out with Tia and has since she was a baby, to see her watching me and I feel like I might have just passed some secret test.

"Thank you, Audrey. You're the best."

I smile as she hugs me tight. "You're welcome, sweet girl."

Breakfast is less chatty than last night but more rushed too. I grab a piece of toast and a coffee as Hudson talks to Mrs. Price. Then we're headed for the door, like this happens every morning, a routine that I've slipped into despite never having shared my morning with a child.

"Did you sleep okay?"

I startle at the question as Hudson and I sit side by side on the drive into the city. He has a driver for this so he can use the time to work, he explained. I get that, I do the same, but I guess for him, it's more important because he needs his spare time for Tia.

"Yes, thank you." I won't admit I had sex dreams about him all night.

"Glad you did. I spent the night imagining you in my bed, and it wasn't conducive to sleep."

His candor surprises me, but I like that he's being so open with me. It doesn't change the past, but it makes me feel easier with what we're doing. Even so, I'm not touching that comment with a twelve-foot pole, so I divert. "Are you free for dinner on Sunday with my parents?"

"Yes, of course. Just give me the details and I'll have Mrs. Price watch Tia."

"You could bring her."

Hudson smooths his tie as he turns sideways to look at me beside him. "Thank you, but I think for this first meeting it might be wise to do it alone. Plus, do your parents even know about Tia?"

I shackle my head. "No, I barely had a chance to explain our marriage, let alone anything else."

"We can bring her next time if this goes well, but I don't want her dragged into an already complex situation until I'm sure it's good for her."

I know what he isn't saying. That he doesn't want Tia to have to face the loss of someone else in her life. It's a gentle reminder, but one I need. "I understand. Thank you for making the time for me."

His hand slides over mine in my lap and he squeezes gently.

"I'll always be there when you need me, Audrey. I'll always make time for you. I promise."

I know he means what he's saying, but the sentiment is so similar to words he whispered in our past, and he broke those promises and me with it, so I can't let myself believe it, even if he does. Yet calling him out seems like the fastest way to destroy this little bit of peace we have right now, and I need that peace more than anything. "I'll text you the details about Sunday."

I hear his sigh and watch frustration crease his brow, but he doesn't lash out or respond, just gives me a slight dip of his head.

The rest of the journey is silent as he answers emails on his phone, and I go over the speech Lincoln sent me for a gala we're all attending in a few weeks. As we pull up to the curb of my building, I look up, surprised that we are here already, and turn to Hudson, but he's already out of the car and coming around to open my door. It's small but it means something to me.

Taking his hand, I step out and release him, tucking my bag over my shoulder and move to walk away.

"Audrey?"

"Yes?"

"Let me know what time you'll be home tonight, and I'll make sure dinner is ready."

I offer him a small smile of thanks and nod as I try to escape the urge to go up on tiptoes and have him kiss me again like he did yesterday.

"Audrey?"

I fight the light feeling as I let my lips tip up at the sides. "Yes?"

"I know you don't believe me, but I meant what I said in the car. I know I let you down in the past, but I've paid for that with what felt like endless years without you. I'll never make that mistake again."

Before I can respond, his head dips, his arm comes around my waist, and he kisses me. It's light, but before I can return the kiss, he's pulling me closer, his other hand cupping the back of my head, so he can angle me exactly how he wants. My toes curl in my pumps and I moan as his teeth scrape my bottom lip. He groans and yanks his head away. Both of us are breathing hard when he rests his forehead against mine.

"Fuck, I missed you."

With that, he lets me go and gets back in the car, but he doesn't pull away until I'm safely inside my building. That is why Hudson is so lethal to my heart, he makes me want every single thing he's offering. Only we're different now. I might be his wife, but I'm not the girl he fell in love with.

11. Hudson

Glancing across the console of the car, I watch Audrey chew her bottom lip with nerves and my dick goes hard, wishing it was me. Friday had been similar to Thursday. I'd cooked a simple dinner of taco bowls and Audrey had spent time making friendship bracelets with Tia while I got a few things done in the office. I hated to work when I was home, but this current project was urgent.

We had a twenty-two-year-old woman who'd married a much older man and was now in a violent, dangerous situation. Lorenzo had been made aware of it by one of his captains and we were arranging for her to be extracted safely. Lorenzo would handle that, and I'd handle the legal side of getting her a divorce and a new life.

Saturday, Audrey spent time with her parents alone, and I went about my usual routine with Tia. Ballet lessons had commenced, despite my lingering concern over Tia having a sniffle still, but she'd been fine and enjoyed it immensely. Audrey had gotten in after dinner and gone to her room, or my room, after saying goodnight to Tia. I hadn't wanted to bother her, but I was concerned about how she was managing everything that was going on.

I stood at the door to my room for a good five minutes trying to figure out what to do. The thought of her in my bed every night, her smooth skin against my sheets, had me gripping my dick and jerking off like a teenage boy with a Victoria's Secret catalog. If I don't get a handle on my need for her soon, I'll probably end up with a repetitive stress injury. Despite all of that, having her here feels good, right. That was fucking terrifying because at some point she'd leave and I'd have to figure out for the second time in my life how to live without her.

Now we are on our way to her parents so I can meet them as their son-in-law for the first time. Audrey was quiet all morning, and I hate seeing her like this. The thought of her hurting guts me in ways I can't explain. It was like her hurting physically pains me.

"Hey, you okay?" I reach for her hand and am pleasantly surprised when she takes it. Her luminous eyes move to me before I glance back to the road. I should have had a driver to bring us, but I wanted this to feel more personal, so I opted to drive my Range Rover.

"Yeah, just a lot going on in my head."

"Anything I can help with?"

Not expecting an answer, I'm slightly shocked by her next words.

"Why didn't you tell me about your mom expecting a baby, and why did you ghost me afterward?"

Shit, we're doing this now. I knew it was coming but had hoped it would be a nice calm conversation at home after dinner and a glass of wine. But I owe her this. Shit, I owe her more. Still gripping her hand, I take the time using the drive to gather my thoughts. Audrey tries to pull her hand away, and I tighten my grip.

"Forget it. It doesn't matter."

"Will you just give me a damn minute to gather my thoughts? I'm going to answer you, but I don't want to just blurt out some meaning-less bullshit. You want the truth, give me a second to put it into words before you react, Belle."

Audrey's eyes widen for a beat before she nods.

"My mom was fifteen when she had me. Her parents kicked her

out, disowning her, and my sperm donor, who was married, wanted nothing to do with us. He gave her five grand and told her to get rid of me. It was tough. From the very beginning, it was always just us. We had nothing, but she gave me all the love I could ever need. As I got older, I became a parent in some ways. My mom was fragile, and I guess I was protective. I worked two jobs to help out and she worked in a hotel as a maid.

"I knew I wanted a better life for us, so I set about making it happen. I got my scholarship and then I met you. Meeting you, Audrey, was like being hit by a falling star. I'd never felt anything like it. When I was around you nothing else mattered and, for the first time, I wanted to be better so I could be worthy of you."

"You were always worthy, Hudson."

Her fingers squeeze mine as I pull into her parents' drive and put the car in park. Angling my body, I unbuckle her seatbelt and pull her across the console and into my lap. Needing her close, wanting her in my arms as I lay all my shame bare for her.

"No, I wasn't even close to being worthy of you and I'm still not. I'm ashamed to say that I hid my home life from you because I was ashamed. I loved my mother, but we had nothing except a crappy one-bedroom flat and, when she got pregnant again by another married asshole that didn't give a fuck about her, I was angry. So damn angry with her, but she was my mom and I'd never abandon her, yet I couldn't find it in me to tell you about how fucked up things were. I was so afraid you'd walk away and I wouldn't have blamed you."

A tear rolls down Audrey's cheek and it guts me that I'm still causing her pain after all this time. I fucking hate that I hurt her and, if I could go back and change one thing in my life, it would be how I handled things with us. I reach up and gently wipe the tear away as I tug her closer, her head on my chest.

I'm sure she can feel how hard my heart is beating in my chest, feel the way my hard dick is pressed against her hip, and I don't care because being here with her feels too good, and I need this, just for a minute. Talking about the past is always hard for me. I have so many complicated emotions, but she deserves the truth.

Her head comes up and those tear-dipped lashes blink up at me. "Is that why you didn't call me?"

"We didn't know Tia had Downs until she was born. Not that it mattered, we both loved her on sight."

Audrey gives me a watery smile. "She is very lovable, like her brother."

I fight not to read into those words as I continue. "I knew my mom would need me more than ever. Tia had some heart issues, but it was my mom's health that sealed it. Her birth was traumatic, and we found out shortly after the birth that she had advanced cervical cancer. Honestly, it was a miracle she'd gone to term, but also why she'd ended up with a C-section. Finding out that I was about to lose my mom, and knowing I was all Tia had, was like getting hit by a bus."

Audrey's palm smooths over my cheek and I close my eyes, savoring every second. "I would have helped if you'd let me."

And there she was, the woman I'd fallen in love with. The woman who'd owned my heart from the first day we'd met. So beautiful inside and out, and she would have given me everything she had and what could I have offered her, apart from the occasional moment of my attention.

"I know you would have, which is why I did what I did. You would have given up everything to help me and I couldn't let you do that. You were too brilliant. Your star was too bright for me to dull it with my drama."

"But I loved you, Hudson."

God, she was killing me, each word a new cut to add to my scarred heart.

Cupping my hands over her cheeks, I lean in closer, craving the touch of her against my lips. I place kisses all over her cheeks, her nose, her eyes, and fight the urge to take her mouth exactly how I want. "I know and, God, I loved you too much to let you. I know I hurt you. I know I broke your heart, and you have no fucking idea how sorry I am for that. If I could go back and change the way I handled things, I would in a heartbeat. But I don't regret setting you free, Belle. You deserved better. You still do."

Audrey lifts her head and I see the fire I love so much in those beautiful brown eyes. "You're right. I deserve a man who'll let me make my own choices, not presume to know what I want or need in my life."

With that, she pulls back and scrambles over to her side of the car. I rush to jump out and open her door, but she beats me to it with a scowl in my direction.

"Now, don't forget I'm the love of your life, so please make this believable for my parents."

I glance at the door, where her mom is waiting with the biggest smile, just like her daughter's. Little does Audrey seem to understand that no acting will be needed. She's the absolute love of my life. Always has been, always will be.

"There you are, the little love birds."

I reach Audrey as she is pulling back from hugging her mother hello and my hand rests on the base of her spine.

"Sorry about that, Mrs. Jones." I'd always thought it strange that Audrey went by Kennedy, but she'd explained it had been at her grandfather's insistence. I didn't know the man personally but from everything I'd heard, he'd been a tyrant in business and a formidable man at home too. Yet Audrey always spoke fondly of him. All I knew was that Judge John Jones must be quite the man to allow it.

Mrs. Jones waved her hand in front of her face as she leaned in to give me a hug. "We don't stand on ceremony here, Hudson. It's Mom or Ruth."

"Thank you, Ruth." I hand her the flowers I'd snagged off the back seat before chasing after my wife. That will never get old.

"Oh, I can see why my daughter fell for you. Handsome and impeccable manners."

I laugh as she takes my arm through hers and pulls me inside the house, Audrey trailing behind us. I turn and reach for her hand, and surprisingly she takes it. Ruth lets go and I see her watching us with a small smile and hope I've passed the first test.

Bending close, I lower my voice to my wife. "You doing okay?"

"Yes, I'm fine."

Her haughty response fills me with something warm. I've always loved her spirited side and will take it over her heartbroken or pensive one any day.

I chuckle and drop a kiss on her cheek before pushing her gently in front of me to hide the erection just being around her gives me. A tiny gasp escapes her when she feels me against her back, only making my situation worse.

"John is taking a short nap, but he'll be awake soon. Why don't you show Hudson around while I check on dinner, Audrey?"

"Is Daddy okay?"

Instantly, I can feel the tension in her body, the change in her tone, and I wish with all my heart I could take this pain away from her. I know what she's facing, and I wouldn't wish it on my worst enemy.

Ruth turns to us, and the dark circles under her eyes tell the story better than words ever will. Audrey is the image of her mother, who is still beautiful despite the grief she wears. "The treatments exhaust him easily, but he's coping."

Audrey pulls away and I stand back, watching the two women together. Knowing I can't do a damn thing but be here for her in any way she needs me.

"Can I do anything, Mom?"

Ruth cups her daughter's cheek. "Sweetheart, you being here helps, and bringing your wonderful husband to join our family has been a huge boost to your father's mood. Knowing you are loved is what he needs."

I move up behind Audrey and cup the back of her neck as she looks up at me, and I turn to Ruth and hope like hell that she can read the truth in my words. "That I can do. Loving your daughter is the easiest thing I've ever done, and I promise you, I'll do everything in my power to make her happy until the day I die."

Ruth blinks tears from her eyes as she squeezes my arm and Audrey just looks at me like I'm her salvation.

"I know, and I can see already how much she loves you."

I wish that were the truth, but for now, I can settle for her not hating my guts.

12. Audrey

"So, tell me about how you two met?"

I glance at Hudson when my dad asks the question. We're eating minted roast lamb, my dad's favorite, but he's hardly touched his. Hudson takes my hand and threads my fingers through his, and I know he's only doing it for show, but right now I need his touch to ground me.

"Well, Audrey and I actually knew each other in college, but I was young and incredibly dumb and let her get away. This time I wasn't going to let that happen."

His eyes find mine as he kisses my palm. I know he's only saying it for my parents' benefit, but after what he told me in the car, my emotions are all over the place.

"Second chance romance. I love that." My mom claps her hands together as she gazes at us like we're Romeo and Juliet without the tragic ending.

"So, all those times you stood in front of me in my courtroom, you were in love with my baby girl?"

My dad cocks his head at Hudson in question, and it almost feels like he can see through our story. Panic takes over, my heart beating like a drum. I don't want my dad to find out it's all a lie.

Hudson must sense my panic because he squeezes my knee under the table. "I was and honestly, sir, I never dreamed she'd give me a second chance, but she did. I'll spend every single day loving her as she deserves to be loved."

The look on Hudson's face almost makes me believe him. God, I want to believe this is real, because the truth is, I never stopped loving him. It was why I spent so long feeding into the hate I thought I felt. It was easier than allowing my broken heart to let go of this man.

Knowing I need to play my part, I lean in and kiss Hudson's cheek as he turns to me with a soft look in his eyes that steals the breath from my lungs.

"All I need is to be loved by you." If he only knew that was true.

"May I ask something of you both?"

Hudson and I both agree as we turn to my father who is watching us with a smile.

"Of course, Daddy. Anything."

"I know it's asking a lot, but would you consider having a second wedding? I'd dearly love to walk my daughter down the aisle to the man she loves."

Stunned by his request and not having a single excuse ready, my throat closes up. How can I do that when none of this is real. Hudson is doing enough for me already.

"Of course, John. It would be our pleasure. Honestly, I'm ashamed of myself for the way it happened the first time. Audrey deserves the wedding of her dreams, and she should have her father walk her down the aisle."

My heart feels like it's lodged someplace in my throat. All my dreams of getting married died with Hudson and now it's like being plunged into an ice bath of lost dreams. So much has happened, so many secrets still stand between us. The people we could hurt with this lie just grows and grows. We're getting in so deep now, and I don't think there's a way out. The worst part is I'm starting to wonder if I want one.

"Daddy, are you sure this won't be too tiring for you?"

"Of course not. Nothing would make me happier than watching you join your life to the man you love."

"Then as long as Hudson is okay with it, we'll plan a second wedding so that everyone we love can attend."

"Excellent. Now, when do we get to meet Tia? I can't wait to have a child in the house again, and she sounds adorable."

I smile at my mom and it's the first genuine one since we walked in the house. "Oh, Mom, you're going to love her. She's sweet and smart and her smile lights up the room. And Hudson is so good with her."

His hand skims up my spine before resting on the back of my neck, and I turn to check he's truly okay with all of this. He's going above and beyond what I asked of him and getting nothing in return. His smile is soft, and his eyes crinkled at the corners, making my tummy flip over. He always had this way of looking at me in the same manner when we were together. Like the outside world didn't exist and it was just the two of us against the world.

"She makes it easy to love her."

He is talking about Tia but looking at me, and it takes everything in me not to lean into him, so I don't fight it, telling myself it's for show. His lips skim my forehead as his arm comes around me. I want to stay like this forever, wrapped in the safety of his arms where nothing can hurt me. Where cancer doesn't exist, where hearts won't break and dreams can't die, but my mother has other ideas and is excited to plan the wedding.

The drive home is quiet, and I can't help but wonder if he's mad at me, so I blurt it out. "Are you mad?"

Hudson pulls into the driveway and shuts off the engine before getting out of the car. His silence weighs heavy, and I feel my defensive anger rising. If he's going to ignore me, then fuck him. I shove past him and he grabs my hand, yanking me back into his arms so I fall against his hard chest.

"Stop being a brat. I'm not mad at all. I just don't want to have all our big conversations in the damn car."

"Well, you could have just said that rather than go all silent, alpha-male on me."

Hudson gives me a sexy smirk, as he pushes open the front door, pushing me in first. "You love it, so don't even deny it."

I'm glad I have my back to him as I answer so he can't see me lie. "I hate it."

Before he can respond, Mrs. Price is coming down the hall and his attention is on her.

"How was she?"

I love how much he worries about Tia but it also hurts in ways I can't explain to him. Seeing him as the father I always knew he'd be is gut-wrenching but also beautiful.

"She was perfect. She's sound asleep so I'll leave you two love birds to it."

I walk into the kitchen as Hudson sees Mrs. Price out and pour myself a sparkling water. Today was a lot to process. His revelations about his mom and how it changes everything I thought about him. I want to be mad still, it's the safest option, but how can I hate him for loving his mom and sister and stepping up into what must have been an awful, situation for him? Yes, he could have handled it better, but I'm not innocent. I could have confronted him and fought harder too.

"Hey, you okay?" His hand brushes my chin as he stands in front of me, and I nod.

"Yes, I'm fine and I'm sorry for snapping at you."

Hudson lifts his brow, and a smirk makes him look like the sexiest sin. "Did Audrey Kennedy just apologize?"

I shove him back, and he loops his arms around my waist and pulls me closer with a chuckle.

"Jackass, and for the record, it's Audrey Carmichael."

His hands feel nice as he strokes my back with the tips of his fingers. "I like the sound of my name with yours."

"Well good job, because we have a wedding to plan." I groan at the thought of it and drop my head to his chest. His hand cups my neck and a shiver of pleasure runs down my spine.

"We don't have to do this if you don't want to, but I thought you'd want to do it."

I lift my head and look at this complicated man who owes me nothing and is still willing to go through with a sham wedding to make my father happy, and a wave of need for him almost lands me on my ass.

"I do want to, but you didn't sign up for this, Hudson."

"I signed up to help you through this, and if this is what you need, this is what we do."

"Thank you, and not just for this but for telling me about your mom and what happened all those years ago. That can't have been easy."

"You deserved the truth. I just wish I'd said it years ago and things might have been different."

Everything in me wants to fall into him and lose myself, but then what? I walk away with my heart torn to shreds again? I wouldn't survive it a second time. I almost didn't the first time. The alternative is unthinkable because having seen Hudson with Tia, I know in my heart he was born to be a father and that's something I just can't give him.

"I guess I should get the ball rolling and make some plans for a wedding." I pull away and put some space between us and he lets his hand fall, a look of disappointment flitting over his face before he masks it.

"Sounds good. Let me know what you need from me."

"I'll put some dates together and email them over to you tomorrow."

"Sounds good."

Hudson purses his lips as if he is trying to stop the words from getting out then knocks the counter with his knuckle. "Good night, Audrey."

This feels off, wrong somehow, and I don't know how to fix it. "Good night, Hudson, and thank you for today. It meant a lot to my parents to see us together." I let a forced laugh out. "I didn't know you were such a good actor."

"I wasn't acting, Audrey. I meant every word I said today."

With that revelation hanging between us, he turns on his heel and heads up the stairs.

That night as I lie in his big bed, his scent on my pillow, I go over every word he uttered today and my belly flutters. I know he only said it to make me feel better, but it doesn't stop me from wanting it all to be true. Hudson has always been it for me and his leaving destroyed me. It's why I built the walls so high, to keep everyone from seeing how broken I was inside. Now I wonder if it was because the thought of loving anyone but him was so alien that even when I thought he'd cheated, I couldn't allow myself the chance. Perhaps this closure was what we both needed. But that feels wrong too.

13. Audrey

"WAIT, LET ME GET THIS STRAIGHT, YOU'RE HAVING A SECOND wedding so your dad can walk you down the aisle but it's fake?"

I glance across at Lottie and nod. We met up at the Littlest Bookworm for a meeting about our kid's dyslexia program and how we could roll it out to smaller bookshops. Now we're walking through the flower market on Lexington. Something about the blooms relaxes me despite the two bodyguards walking behind us. Linc is still overprotective of his wife, and she lets him because she knows he needs it.

"Yes."

"Why would you do that?"

"Because my dad put us on the spot and Hudson said yes."

"Hudson agreed?"

"Before I did."

"That man is still in love with you."

I stop at a stand filled with Alstroemerias and look at my friend, my mouth agape. "He is not."

"Denial. It's classic."

Shaking my head, I begin walking again. "It's not denial. It's truth."

The Enemy

"So, he's staying married to you, and re-marrying you so that you can make your dad happy just because you asked?"

I shrug. "Hudson's a good man."

"Hudson is a good man. He's also head over heels for you, and you can deny it all you want but you feel the same way."

"It doesn't matter if I do, nothing can come of this."

Lottie stops and grabs my arm. "Wait, you love him?"

Biting my lip, I look away before nodding. "I don't think I ever stopped."

Lottie squeals and her bodyguards jump before she waves them away. "Audrey, this is huge. You've always said how much you hate him."

"I know, but that was when I thought he cheated on me. When he explained everything about his mom and Tia's birth, my anger kind of died and now I'm left with the awful realization that I still love him."

"Why awful?"

"Because it would never work between us now. He deserves better than half a woman who would think so badly of him."

"Oh, bullshit. Why would you say that crap?"

Now it's my turn to stop walking. "It's not crap."

"It's utter and complete crap. You're smart, kind, beautiful, successful. Any man would be lucky to have you."

I shake my head. "You don't understand."

And how could she, nobody knows. I hide myself away under a veneer of perfection. I'm a fraud and it's exhausting.

"Then make me understand because from where I'm standing, we have two people who love each other who are faking the fact that they're faking being in love instead of going after what they want."

"I can't have children."

The words spill out of me, as if I can't hold them in any longer and it feels like a relief to say it out loud after all this time.

"Oh, honey, I'm sorry. Can I ask?"

"I need coffee and cake for this conversation."

"Great idea and now I don't want to puke every two minutes, I can enjoy it too."

We head out of the flower market and over to a little coffee shop called Java Junkies which do the best blueberry muffins on the planet. We order and find a table near the back corner as our shadows station themselves two tables over and growl at anyone who comes close. It's normal for me, I've had close protection for years, but I know Lottie is still finding it strange.

"So, do you want to talk about it?"

"I do actually, and that's a first."

Lottie covers my hand with hers and I feel so lucky to have her in my life as my family.

"I told you about what happened with Hudson and I, and how I went to find him, but I didn't mention that I was pregnant at the time."

I hear Lottie suck in a breath and somehow watching her emotions helps me to keep mine from drowning me in grief. "Well, I saw what I saw. I was crying so hard on the drive back that I was in a car accident. It was nothing major, just a bump, but I lost the baby. I was devastated and Lincoln is the only person who knows because I called him after the accident. It's why he's so hard on Hudson."

"Oh, Audrey, that's awful. You poor thing. But that shouldn't mean you can't have a successful pregnancy next time around."

I know she's being kind, but it still hurts to have that hope flashed in from of your eyes even for a second. "No, I can't. After about a year, my periods were either non-existent or really light, so I went to see a specialist. He diagnosed me with Asherman's Syndrome. It's where the uterine lining scars, and it can cause infertility. The doctor said the likelihood of me getting pregnant was almost nil."

"God, that's awful."

I huff a laugh and take a bite of my muffin to hide the pain I still feel. If I hadn't been pregnant then I wouldn't have had the procedure which probably caused my condition. It's hard not to be bitter about that, but Hudson has no idea.

"Does Hudson know any of this?"

I shake my head. "No, what's the point? He feels bad enough about what he did and telling him solves nothing."

"It might help you both if you're honest with him, and then you can have a healthy start and make something real out of the ashes of the past."

"I don't know. He hasn't said outright that he even wants this to be real."

"Have you?"

"No."

Lottie gives me her 'mom' look and I roll my eyes at her. "That look doesn't work on me."

"You need to tell him and stop hiding."

"How can you say that to me after what I just told you?"

"Because I love you like the sister I never had. What happened is awful, but it doesn't mean you can't have a future with the man who loves you and who you love."

Her words hit me hard. Could I have it all even now or is it a pipe dream that will blow up in my face?

I can't deny I want to be with Hudson. These last three days not seeing him or Tia have been horrible. My apartment, which I'd once loved, now feels too quiet and cold. I miss the noisy dinners and the dolls strewn about and the paintings on the fridge. How has my life turned upside down in just four days? "What if it doesn't work out?"

"What if it does? Are you going to let the fear of one outshine the hope of the other?"

"He might not even want me."

"Will you stop? He wants you and since when have you ever stood back and not gone after something you want? You're Audrey fucking Kennedy. You don't wait, you conquer."

"So, I should conquer Hudson?"

"Well, I'm not sure conquering him will work. Something tells me that man wears the pants in the bedroom, but I do think you should climb him like a tree and then ride him until you can't see straight."

I scowl at Lottie and throw my napkin at her. "I think I prefer you meek and mild."

"No, you don't."

"No, I don't."

The truth is, I love how confident Lottie is now. She blossomed and, in turn, softened the harsh edges of my cousin. They make each other better. I'm just not sure Hudson and I do that. But there is a part of me that wants to find out, even though it terrifies me.

Lottie laughs and we move onto the subject of the wedding plans. We have three weeks to pull this off after Hudson agreed to a date last night over text messages.

"So, let's do this. What do you need me to do?"

We set about making a list of everything we need and, as we're close, we head back to the flower market to look at ideas for the bouquet and arrangements. Usually, thinking about my infertility leaves me in a pit of depression but today I don't feel that. Talking to Lottie about what happened is freeing. It changes nothing but it makes me realize that my happiness doesn't have to be tied to my ability to have a child.

As we round the corner into the section of the market with roses, I see a familiar figure leaning against the door, one hand shoved in his pocket. As he sees me, he pushes off and walks toward me, a sexy smile on his face.

"Hudson, what are you doing here?"

He takes the bags from my hands without even asking and kisses my cheek, his warm, soft lips making my skin tingle.

"Lottie sent me a text and said you were picking flowers, so I thought I'd join you. Is that okay?"

I glance at Lottie who is walking backwards. "I just remembered I have that thing I need to do. I'll call you later."

That devious little minx. "You'd better."

"Is it okay that I'm here? I don't want to intrude."

The Enemy

I angle my head up to him, before lifting on my toes and kissing his full lips. He's caught off guard but as his arm comes around me, anchoring me to his chest, he quickly takes back control. He presses his lips to me harder as if he can't get close enough and a whimper escapes me, as I clutch at his jacket. His hand moves up my back before tangling into my hair. It's like the leash has snapped and all of the caged passion is free. I move against him, and his erection is like stone against my belly. A growl rumbles up Hudson's chest and I feel it everywhere. My panties are soaked, and the need to feel him inside me is overwhelming.

With a nip to my bottom lip, Hudson breaks the kiss as we both try and catch our breaths.

"What was that for, wife?"

"I missed you."

Hudson smiles against my lips. "You missed me, huh?"

I nod because admitting it out loud again makes me feel vulnerable.

"I missed you too."

My fingers slip over his jaw. "You did?"

"Every day."

I know he only means since we got married but I still like to hear it. "So, I was thinking while we're pretending to be married maybe we could, you know, take advantage of the perks."

"Oh, and what are those?"

I can feel the heat on my cheeks, and glance away from his eyes.

Hudson doesn't let me get away with that, though, and lifts my chin with his knuckle. "How do you own a sex club and you can't even say the words?"

"Shut it."

"Sounds like that mouth needs to be kept occupied."

I love this dominant flirty side of him. "Oh yeah? What do you have in mind?"

"How about we finish this conversation in private?"

I look around to see people watching us and a blush crawls over my neck. I may not court the public eye but, with my wealth, I'm well known, and we've attracted a crowd. "Good idea."

"While I'm here, do you want to look at flower choices?"

Hudson takes my hand and turns me to the display of roses, and it feels nice to be here with him. "Yes, that would be nice. Do you have a preference?"

"No, I got everything I need."

"How about roses? They're classic, elegant."

"And what else would Belle choose for her wedding to the beast."

My lips split into a smile at his words but now I know he's less beast and more prince, but the truth is I love them both. I just have to decide if I'm brave enough to go after it.

"Exactly. How about red roses?"

"Perfect."

"But I want to ask Tia before I confirm."

Hudson frowns. "You don't need to do that."

"Don't you want me to involve her?"

"No, it's not that. She's excited as hell about wearing a real princess dress, but I don't want to force you into including her."

"I want her included. She's your sister and I want her to enjoy this experience."

Hudson cups my cheek, and I can't help but imagine what it would be like if this were all real. "Thank you."

"My pleasure." And it really is. Tia is a joy to be around.

We get home around six, but what we started in the flower market is on hold as Hudson had to take some calls in the car and I had to speak with our accountant about the new financial structure for the news show, which is now up and running under new management. It's my pet project and I was so excited about it, but now it seems like it couldn't have come at a worse time.

Tia is a bundle of chatter when we walk through the door, and Hudson throws me a smile with an I 'told you so' look. I don't mind Tia's excitement. In fact, I find it infectious.

The Enemy

Over dinner, she's telling me about the dress she wants to wear and describing all the details and I have an idea.

"How about you come with us when I go and choose my dress? We can get your dress then too."

Lottie would be my maid of honor, with Norrie, Eden, and Amelia as bridesmaids, with Tia as flower girl.

I look to Hudson, who's gone still. "I don't know if that's a good idea. Tia hasn't met them, and it will be busy. I don't know if it will be good for her."

Hudson, I'm starting to see, is wildly overprotective of her and I wonder if he thinks he's protecting her when he's actually stifling her a little out of love.

"Why wouldn't it be good for her?"

"Please, Huddy." Tia has her hands in a prayer position as she gives him a look that would make me want to slay dragons so she could get what she wanted.

"Can we talk in the kitchen, Audrey?"

I stand and wink at Tia as I follow Hudson from the room.

He takes my elbow as he glares at me. "What are you doing?"

"Including your sister in our wedding."

"Our fake wedding. I don't want her meeting everyone and getting attached and then getting her heart broken."

"Why would she get her heartbroken?"

"Not everyone is kind to her Audrey. Some people are downright awful, and I can't stand to see her hurt."

I frown at his words, hating that he's witnessed that kind of thing. "You know Lottie and the girls would never treat her with any kind of negativity or hate. They'll see what I see, which is a beautiful child excited to wear a pretty dress."

"And what about the others?" He throws his arm up. "The assistants in the shop? What if they upset her or she does something to embarrass you and I'm not there to step in?"

Suddenly I see what this is about and if I wasn't already halfway in love with him, I would be now. He wants to spare me any embarrassment from someone judging Tia, and Tia from ever having to feel any kind of rejection from a society that isn't always kind. God, this man. When he loves, he loves hard.

"First, nothing Tia could do would embarrass me."

"But..."

I hold my finger over his lips and give him the full Audrey Kennedy glare. "Nothing she could do. Second, if anyone upsets her or even lifts a brow at her that I don't think is in anything but kindness, I'll ruin them."

Hudson nips at my finger over his lips and I try and hide my smirk as a curl of pleasure snakes between my legs.

"I promise you, Hudson, I'll protect her as if she was my own. She's safe with me. Let her go and I promise I'll keep her heart safe."

Hudson sighs and dips his head in a nod.

Running my hands up his chest, I lift and nip his earlobe, causing a hiss from his lips as he grasps my hips and pulls me close.

"Thank you."

"Audrey?"

"Yes?"

"When Tia is asleep, I want you in my bed, naked."

My body hums with desire at his demand. "Oh, is that so?"

His hands grip my ass hard as he pulls me against his hard cock, his lips find my neck and he runs his tongue lightly over my pulse, as my eyes close in pleasure.

"It is so. I want you naked and wet and ready to take my cock. I want you squirming and desperate for my tongue on your clit. I want you begging."

I squeeze my legs together to ease the ache his words are causing. "I'm Audrey Kennedy, I beg for no man."

His hand moves from my ass as he strokes up my ribs, skimming my breasts before he cups my throat in a loose hold. His breath is warm against my neck, and I shiver as it tickles my skin.

"You're Audrey Carmichael, and you beg for your husband."

He releases me with a kiss on my cheek and I have to catch

The Enemy

myself on the counter to stop myself from collapsing into a puddle on the floor. God, that man can talk dirty, and with a few words, he has me wanting to crawl on my hands and knees for him.

It's dangerous and delicious and I want him more than I've ever wanted anything. Now, I just have to survive playing dolls with his sister before she goes to bed without combusting into a heaping pile of need on the floor.

14. Hudson

I can barely contain my desperation to race after her as Audrey walks up the stairs to what I now think of as her room. The anticipation is so heightened that every movement causes the fabric of my pants to scrape against my aching cock.

Meeting her at the market after a text from Lottie had been an impulse, but I knew it was the right decision when she kissed me, shocking me with a move I know Audrey doesn't ever make.

Audrey, that rare beauty, has no need to make moves on men and, despite how forward and confident she is, I also know she prefers to take a more submissive role when it comes to sex. Perhaps because she likes to cede power and just enjoy the moment, tired from all the huge decisions she makes in her daily life. I think it's just who she is. She was always like it before, but now it's like she craves the release of submission.

Checking the locks on the doors and making sure the security alarm is armed, I head upstairs. When I pop my head in on Tia, she's sprawled diagonally across her bed, her favorite stuffed animal looped over her arm. Tucking her in, I stroke her hair from her face and hope I'm doing the right thing, letting her go with Audrey and her friends to get her dress. I've always been her only protector, the only person to keep the bad away from her, and now I'm trusting a woman who has every right to hate me for the way I treated her, who could use my vulnerability to seek revenge. Yet I don't believe for one second Audrey would do that. She's too kind, too moral, to ever use a child, and I see the way she looks at Tia with the same soft look she used to look at me.

Closing the door, I head to the room I'm using and take a quick shower. Ignoring my straining erection, I dry off and dress in loose cotton sweatpants. I don't bother with a shirt, I want no clothing getting between me and what I want, and that's to bury myself in the woman who consumes my every thought and make her feel pleasure like never before.

I don't knock as I enter my room. As my gaze moves to the bed, hot need courses through me. "You take instruction well, Belle."

Audrey is lying on the bed naked, her dark hair splayed on the white pillow, her chest heaving with each breath she takes. God, she's fucking breathtaking. Pre-cum leaks from the tip of my cock and I swear I could come from merely watching her lie there.

I feel her eyes moving over me hungrily as I step toward the bed. The folds of her pussy are glistening with the evidence of her desire, and I want to taste every inch of her body, but not yet. I want to take my time.

"Open your legs for me."

Standing beside the bed, I look down on her smooth skin, her breasts high and round with peaked nipples begging for my lips. Her flat belly quivers, and I know it's anticipation she feels.

Audrey does as I ask without delay and I drop to my knees beside the bed, running my finger through her soaked pussy, gathering up her juices as she arches her back and moans. Her eyes are on me as I bring the finger to my lips and taste her pleasure. Sweet and tangy, she's perfection, and I don't know how I've gone so long without the taste of this woman on my lips.

"I could live off the taste of you, so sweet, so perfect."

"Hudson, please."

"What, my sweet, Belle? What do you need?"

"I want you to touch me."

I'll always give this woman what she wants but she needs to trust me, to give her what she needs too. "Do you trust me, Audrey?"

Her dark eyes are heavy with desire as she looks up at me, her full bottom lip caught between her teeth. "Yes."

"Then let me give you what I know you need."

Her nod is hardly consent, but in this moment between us, it's all I need from her. "Spread those pussy lips and show your husband what's his."

Audrey was built for sex, for sin and, as she runs her hand down her body and does as I ask, I almost explode with pleasure. Hot, pink, and soaked, she doesn't hold back.

"Fuck yourself with your fingers."

Her breath hitches and I wonder if this is too intimate for her, but she does as I ask, sliding her pointer and middle finger inside her hot cunt. A groan tears from my throat and I palm my cock, trying to ease the ache, the desperate need to bury myself inside her.

Bending my head, I catch her nipple between my teeth, biting down gently as her spine arches her front against me. I chuckle at her wanton need and suck her into my mouth, feasting hungrily on the tight bud as she continues to fuck herself as I watch.

Her body begins to writhe, and I know she's close, so I lift my head. "Stop."

Her gaze snaps to mine and I can see the fire in them, and God but I love it. This woman was born to conquer kingdoms, her beauty meant to launch ships, and here she lies in my bed, waiting for permission from me to come.

"Good girl."

I stand and shove my joggers down my thighs, kicking them off as I palm my dick and stroke once. Audrey sits up on her elbows, her gaze on my cock, as she licks her lips.

"Come here."

The Enemy

I step back and she moves to stand, but I stop her. "No, get on your hands and knees and crawl to your husband."

A spark of defiance flickers in her eyes, making me want to fall to my knees and worship this woman for all eternity. I force myself to remain still and hold her gaze until she does exactly as I ask.

She's as graceful as a cat as she crawls her way across the carpet to me. My palm strokes down her silky hair as I cup her cheek and force her to look up at me. My fingers skim her lips as I pull her bottom lip open. "Stick out your tongue, beautiful."

Her gaze bounces to my cock as I grip my length and coat her lips with my pre-cum, before sliding my dick along her tongue. Pleasure tingles along my spine and I groan at the hot, wet, feel of her mouth on me. "Suck."

She does, hollowing her cheeks and taking me as deep as she can, her tongue a delicate, delicious torture on my crown. My fingers fist in her hair as I pump my hips lightly, unable to deny the pleasure she gives me. Seeing her on her knees for me as she gives me this trust, this heady pleasure, is something I'll never forget and will always treasure.

As the intensity builds and her moans vibrate down my cock, I pull her away. A whimper tears from her throat and I smile, pleased with how much she enjoys sucking me off. "You're incredible."

I lift her to her feet and scoop her into my arms before capturing her lips with a wild, starving kiss. I hold her in my arms at the edge of the bed as we kiss like the world is about to end. Her body writhes against me, the hard peaks of her nipples are a torture against my chest. We are one, and here we're equal as we chase the feeling only we can give each other.

Sex has never been like this with anyone but her, and I know she feels the same. But I promised her she'd beg, and I'll make her because she needs this too.

Placing her down, I kneel between her legs and push her knees apart. Her inner thighs are soaked with her juices, and I want to lick every single drop up. Bending my head, I kiss her knee, worshipping her as I make my way higher. Licking at the sweetness coating her thighs, her fingers card through my hair.

"I've dreamed of this, Belle. Dreamed of the taste of your cunt on my tongue."

"Hudson, please. I need you."

Flattening my tongue, I lick her pussy from the entrance to her clit, burying my head in her pretty pussy and dragging her pleasure out of her. Her legs shake as I suck her clit into my mouth, flicks of my tongue making her hips buck as she seeks out more.

"Beg, me, Audrey. Beg your husband to let you come."

"Please, Hudson, I'm begging you, make me come."

A smile pulls at my lips before I dive back between her legs and eat her cunt like she's my last meal. I push two fingers inside her tight pussy and curl them as she squeezes them. Her pleasure feeds my own and I know the sheet beneath me is soaked from my leaking cock.

"Come for your husband, Audrey."

Her back arches, and I hold her down as a low keening sound erupts from her throat. Her thighs clamp around my ears and she soaks my chin with her climax. I drink her down as the tension leaves her body limp and satiated on my sheets.

Sitting up, I watch her gazing at me with soft eyes as I wipe my chin with the back of my hand. "Such a good girl."

"I want you."

She reaches for me, and I can deny her nothing. I wrap my fist around my cock and brace myself on one hand as I lean close. "Are you protected?"

"Yes, and I have regular physicals because of the club."

I don't want to consider the club or the other men she might have slept with because it makes me want to tear any man who has had the privilege of seeing her like this apart.

"I'm clean and I want to fuck you raw. Are you okay with that?"

"Yes."

My muscles shake as I swipe the head of my dick through her

pussy lips. Her hands reach for my biceps as I push inside slowly, savoring every inch that she takes. She's so tight and hot, I can hardly stand the urge to just pound into her and take the pleasure, but I'd rather die than hurt her and I'm not a small man in any sense.

A whimper falls from her lips.

"You're doing so well, beautiful. Look."

Her eyes fall to where we're joined, and I feel the glide of wetness increase, allowing me to sink into her to the hilt.

"Fuck."

"I need you to move, Hudson."

I dip my head and take her mouth in a hot kiss as my hips move and begin to fuck every bad memory about us out of her head. I want her to be so full of me, of us, that she can't see or feel anything else. Her legs lock around my back and I lift her ass in my hands as I sit back on my heels.

Watching the way her body convulses and shudders around my cock is my new favorite thing. We stare into each other's eyes, sweat pouring down my back as I fuck her hard and fast. Even knowing I won't last, I can't stop. It's like finally having her again has unleashed a demon inside me and only she can exorcise it. "So damn good."

Her pussy clenches around my cock and my body locks. Every muscle and sinew was electrified by her. I feel the blood coursing through me. Everything seems brighter, stronger, better when we're together.

"Oh, God, I'm... I'm going to come."

I reach for her clit and apply just the right amount of pressure as if I know her body better than my own and she cries out. I cover her mouth with mine and drink down her climax as she spasms around me, dragging my own orgasm from me, my balls drawing up and my spine tingling with release. I bury my head against her neck and moan her name. My hot come spills deep inside her.

Sagging against her, I roll us so I don't crush her and bring her into my arms. I know I need to get up and clean her up, but I just want to enjoy this moment before reality crashes back into us both.

"Thank you for trusting me with your pleasure."

Audrey huffs a laugh against my chest as she snuggles deeper. "It was worth it."

Audrey always likes to come across as untouchable and aloof, and I respect that. She gives the world what she needs them to see, for her to live her life on her terms. But the fact that she's curled against me like a contented kitten shows more about her trust in me than she can imagine, and I will never not treasure the fact that she lets me see this part of her.

"So, what now?"

I look down to where her hand is resting on my chest and see her watching me with a look of uncertainty, which is so unlike her.

"What do you mean?"

"Well, we're fake married, getting a fake second ceremony for my parents, and now we're sleeping together. Don't you think this kind of complicates things?"

"First, we aren't fake married, we're actually married. Second, the thing for your parents is something we can do to make them smile. And last, us sleeping together was inevitable."

"Maybe, but so much has happened, so much hurt. I'm concerned if we get too deep, one of us will get hurt when all of this is over."

If I have my way, nobody is walking away from anything, but I know she'll run if I suggest that. Audrey is skittish and still keeping secrets and until she trusts me with those, we don't stand a chance. Lucky for her I'm a patient man.

"How about we take each day as it comes and carry on as we are? Being with me and Tia isn't so bad, is it?"

Her nose wrinkles as her fingers play over my nipple, making my dick twitch back to life.

"Tia is the best, and I adore spending time with her. She's like a walking dose of sunshine on a cloudy day. You, however, are a giant pain in my ass."

I move fast, rolling to pin her to the bed with my body as she giggles, and it's like a dose of pure serotonin being pumped into my veins. Will I ever not love this woman? I know the answer to that, but I need to keep a clear head for Tia's sake.

"Pain in your ass, hey?"

"Yep, but also kind of sweet and cute, too."

I drop my head and kiss her slowly, tenderly, trying to convey everything I feel for her. "Sweet and cute aren't good for my reputation, Belle."

"It's okay, Hudson. Your secret is safe with me."

This I know, but as I swing her up into my arms and carry us into the shower to get us dirtier before we clean up, I wonder if my heart is as safe.

15. Audrey

THIS WEEK HAS BEEN PERFECT. HUDSON AND I SEEM TO HAVE found a rhythm that includes daily orgasms and, yes, that's plural. I haven't bothered to go home to my apartment. We have so much to do to organize this wedding ceremony, in such a short space of time, that it seems silly to go home just to spend all night on the phone. This way I get to wake up to his head between my legs and I couldn't be happier about it.

Sex with Hudson was always fantastic, but this is next level. We connect in a way that feels like he can read my every need. And he makes me feel safe enough to be myself without the worry of judgment.

"Audrey, are you almost ready to go?"

I lift my eyes to see his reaction when he steps into the bedroom we now share, and he doesn't disappoint. His footsteps falter and he stills in the doorway as his gaze moves over my body with a slow hungry perusal.

"Wow, you look heart-stopping beautiful."

I blush and dip my head to see the outfit I chose for the dinner my parents are throwing us. I wanted to look beautiful for Hudson tonight. He's doing so much for me and my family and I want him to know how much it means to me. My dress is a one-shoulder, sleeveless, green velvet with a thigh slit, and a high waist that showcases all my curves while remaining elegant enough to be around my parents.

"Do you like it?"

Hudson shakes his head, as he walks toward me and takes my hand, spinning me in a full circle.

"No, like isn't a strong enough word. But then you'd look beautiful in a Target bag."

I raise my brow and smirk. "Target, really?"

Hudson rolls his eyes and pulls me against him. "Fine, Dior." He strokes a finger over the curve of my breast, making me shiver with desire for him. "This is my favorite color on you."

I glance up and find his eyes on me. "I know."

We stand entranced by each other, and I wonder, not for the first time, how I'll survive walking away from him.

"We should go. I don't want to give Lincoln a reason to hate me more than he already does."

Guilt blooms in my chest as I nod and grab my bag from the dressing table. My wedding and engagement ring twinkle in the light and it shocks me how quickly I've grown to love the weight of the gold against my skin.

I should tell Hudson everything. He has a right to know, but I can't stand the thought of him looking at me like I'm broken. I just want to enjoy this time we have.

We're quiet on the drive over to my parents' place. It's not awkward or forced, but nice. We park and walk to the door of my parents' home, where a uniformed member of our household staff is taking coats.

"You okay?"

I turn and smile at him as he takes my fingers and kisses my palm. "I am. Just thinking about my dad. This is a lot for him, and I don't want to tire him out."

"I'm sure your mom has her eye on him, and if we see him getting tired, we can cut things short."

"Thank you, Hudson, for everything."

He looks so handsome in his charcoal grey suit and vest, his white shirt and green tie matching my dress. But it's the way he looks at me that makes the butterflies in my belly scatter.

"It's my absolute pleasure, Belle."

Taking his arm, we head inside. My mother greets us both with a hug and tells me that my dad will be down shortly. Aunt Heather is beside her, as I know she will be when the time comes and my dad leaves us.

"Congratulations, you two. Audrey, you look stunning and, Hudson, I have no clue why Lincoln calls you the beast, but my boy must have salt in his eyes."

I stiffen at my aunt's words, but Hudson merely kisses her cheek and laughs.

"Don't believe everything you hear about me, Mrs. Kennedy."

"Oh, tosh, call me Heather. And I'm the mother of two boys, I haven't listened to much he's said since he hit puberty."

"Mother, can you not join the dark side for once, please?"

We turn to see Lincoln and Lottie walking towards us as Aunt Heather laughs and walks away with my mom to look at something in the kitchen.

"Carmichael." My cousin greets Hudson and holds out his hand. It's a sign of peace, and I'm grateful for it.

Hudson takes it. "Coldwell." He turns to Lottie with a warm smile as I greet Lincoln. "Lottie, you look well. How are you?"

"She's perfectly fine, thank you, Carmichael, so save your concern."

"Lincoln." I admonish, but Hudson shakes his head and wraps an arm around me.

"It's fine. I understand him wanting to protect the woman he loves."

Lottie fans herself, her eyes widening, and I shake my head with a grin.

"Do you really?"

"Yes, I do. You'd crawl through broken glass to make them smile and die a thousand deaths to keep them safe."

"Exactly."

They stare off for a second that stretches before Lincoln laughs and punches Hudson on the shoulder in some weird male bonding routine. "You're not the asshole I thought you were, Hudson."

"So happy you think so, Lincoln. Your opinion means everything to me."

Ryker comes up between them and grabs both men around the shoulders. "We bonding or what?"

Eden, who looks radiant in a red strapless satin dress and the most adorable baby bump, rolls her eyes. "Ignore him, he's just happy because my father has agreed to build him a custom bike."

As Beck, Xander, and Amelia arrive next, followed by Harrison and Norrie, the men seem to splinter off into a little huddle with Hudson at the center.

"Stop worrying."

I turn away from Hudson, as he throws me a wink, to look at Amelia. "I just need them to remember he's doing me a favor and not give him the third degree."

Norrie hands me a glass of Champagne. "Relax, the boys are just looking out for you."

"And Hudson can handle himself," Lottie adds.

"I guess." I cast him one last look before giving my friends my attention.

"So, what's new with everyone? I feel like I haven't seen you in ages."

"That's because you're too busy getting all the orgasms from Mr. Hottie over there."

"Norrie!"

"What? Am I wrong? Are you not getting some prime dick every night?"

A smile teases my lips, and they all begin to laugh.

"I knew it," Amelia hisses. "Tell me he's good. He has that energy that says he leaves a woman gasping for more."

"Don't you have two of the hottest men on the planet panting after you every second of the day?"

Amelia shrugs and gives a little smirk as she looks over at Xander and Beck, who as if they feel her gaze, look up, and the heat between them almost melts the clothes off my back.

"Yeah, I do, but I want that for my girls too." She looks back at me. "And you're the last one standing."

"Listen, I appreciate that, but this is just sex. Good sex, but nothing more."

"Good sex?"

I roll my lips and nod at Eden.

"With your startlingly hot husband."

I repeat the nod to Norrie. "Yes."

"And no feelings are involved at all?"

I glare at Lottie. "Is this some kind of comedy routine?"

"You started it with that ridiculous comment."

"Why is it ridiculous?"

Norrie looks up at me and props her hands on her hips. It's amazing how none of these girls are afraid of me anymore. When we met, they all gave me a healthy dose of respect, and were slightly intimidated by me, but not now. Now I get all the sass and I love them for it.

"Because, young lady, you only have to see the way you two look at each other to see how much love there is between you."

"Rubbish. What you see is lust."

A hand lands on my shoulder and I spin to see my dad looking gray and frail in a suit that now hangs off his thin frame.

"My darling daughter, might I impart some parental wisdom?"

The Enemy

I give my friends a look that promises retribution and they all start to laugh.

"I preferred it when you were all scared of me," I hiss, before turning to hug my dad. "Hey, Daddy. Yes, of course, lay that wisdom on me."

"From a man who has been married for over thirty years, let me tell you that when you love someone deeply it's impossible to hide it. I see the way Hudson looks at you."

"How does he look at me?" My heart is pounding out of my chest in case we've been busted and I'm about to break my dad's heart.

"Like I look at your mother. From the first day we met, I knew I'd marry her and she'd be the love of my life. I see that between you two and it makes my heart soar."

A hand comes around my waist, and I feel the heat of him at my back and I automatically sink into the comfort her offers me.

"When you know, you know. Right, John?"

"Absolutely, son."

Hudson shakes my father's hand and I wish with all my heart that this was real and not done because my father is sick. That we could be that couple, like my friends, and have a future, but all I have promised is right now.

"Ah, I see Xander. I want to ask him about his new film. Excuse me."

My dad wanders off, and I bite back the tears as I watch him. Even in the last few weeks, he seems to have shrunk. A sob lodges in my throat and I feel like I can't breathe.

"Come with me."

Before I know it, Hudson is pulling me from the room and into the garden. A shiver slides over me, but he pulls me close and holds me against him as I let the night sky soothe me.

"You're going to be alright, Audrey. Just breathe with me."

His hands cup my face and I keep my eyes locked on his as we breathe in and out until the stone in my chest melts away.

Then his arms come around me as I lean into him, taking his

strength because my own is failing me. "How do I say goodbye to him, Hudson? How do I carry on without the man, who taught me to ride a bike, looking out for me?"

"You do it by remembering all of the small moments. You wake up each day and let the pain wash over you. It will hurt and it will feel like you lost your anchor, but every day the pain will become bearable as the pain turns from a scab into a scar. Then you'll begin to remember them with a smile."

I pull away and look at him. "Is that how it is for you?"

He nods. "Yes. I miss her every day and I still go to tell her things, only to remember she isn't around to listen. But I tell her anyway, and I remember that she's a part of me, of Tia too, and I honor her by being the best person I can for my sister."

"That's beautiful but I don't have Tia to keep me going. I feel like I'm standing in quicksand just waiting for the inevitable moment when it drags me under and suffocates me."

"You have your mom, and your cousin, as awful as he is."

I laugh as a smile crinkles his eyes.

"And you have me. I know I wasn't there for the last few years and that's on me, but I'm here now, and I'm not going anywhere. As long as you need me, I'll be right by your side."

"I need to tell you something." This isn't the time or the place but I can't help it. I need to get this out before I change my mind.

"You can tell me anything, Belle."

"When you left, I didn't know it, but I was pregnant."

Hudson seems to freeze, his gaze looking vacant as he takes in my words and then he shakes his head, stepping back with a frown. "What?"

"I was pregnant. I found out a week after you left. It's why I came looking for you."

His hands skim his hips, and he looks ashen. "You had my baby?"

I shake my head as I reach for him and, by some miracle, he lets me take his hands. "No."

He snatches his hands away angrily, and my temper flares.

The Enemy

"You got rid of my baby without even mentioning it to me?"

I fold my arms, my anger a comfortable cloak around me as I give him a haughty look. "If you remember rightly, I thought you were shacked up with your baby momma already."

Hudson scrubs a hand down his face and turns his back to me and I let my front fall for just a second. This isn't fair, I can't torture him with this. "I lost the baby."

He spins so fast that I step back, but he follows until he has me in his arms.

"This is all my fault. If I'd spoken to you, told you about my mom and Tia, we could be a family right now." He sounds distraught as he cups my head to his chest.

"You don't know that. Miscarriages happen all the time."

"Maybe, but we would've been together. I could've held you and loved you."

Tears sting my eyes as I rise up on tiptoes and kiss him, and I can feel the grief and regret. He kisses me like I'm a life raft, and we're both drowning. Nothing about us feels fake, it never has. Hudson and I have always been end-game, except our game seems to have been called at halftime.

"Hey, love birds, dinner is ready."

I wrench my lips away from Hudson and nod at Lincoln. "Be there in a second." Hudson is breathing hard as I lean my forehead against his. "We need to go inside."

"I know. Can you give me a minute?"

I nod and kiss his cheek. I have no idea what I might have done to us with my ill-timed confession but I do know it's well overdue.

16. Hudson

Dinner is a blur. Physically, I was present but mentally I was still back in the garden, shuddering under the weight of the bombshell Audrey dropped on my head. I can tell from the way she keeps shooting me distressed looks that she didn't mean to confess everything like she had. Maybe she planned for me to never find out.

I try and tune into something Harrison is saying but all I really want to do is get out of here and talk to Audrey. I feel her hand on my thigh, and I know, from the tentative touch, that this isn't an attempt to seduce me. She's seeking reassurance, and that I can give her. I fold my hand over hers and squeeze gently while shooting her a light smile. Hoping I can convey that it will be okay when I'm not sure I believe that anymore.

It's not anger at her that simmers beneath my skin, it's anger at myself. If I'd just told her what was going on in my life, things might have been so different. Instead, we're two people with a chasm between us.

Thankfully, the evening wraps up quickly. John is exhausted and you don't need to be a doctor to see how fast he's fading. I watched my own mother succumb to this awful disease, and knowing what

Audrey faces, I'd give my fortune to save her from this pain, but I can't and it's killing me.

"You guys going to come to the club with us?"

I turn to Beck as he speaks and catch Audrey shaking her head, before looking at me.

"I'm exhausted. But, Hudson, you can go if you want."

Cocking my head, I try to read her expression. Is she wanting me to go so she can have some space or is she giving me an out somehow from the conversation that is looming? Either way, it's not happening. "No, I'm going to take my wife home."

I pull her close as we stand in the lounge as Heather rushes around to gather coats. Audrey doesn't fight me but leans into my touch and I let some of the tension inside me go. We can get past this. We just need to talk it through.

This last week has been perfect, everything I ever dreamed of, and while I know she's skittish still, what we have is special and I think deep down she knows it.

"Fair enough. We'll see you at Ruin later this week for the party?"

I look at Audrey as I wait for her answer, and she nods. She hasn't mentioned a party at the club, but we don't really talk about Club Ruin. I'm in no way a prude. Fuck, there's nothing more I like than making Audrey beg for my cock, but the thought of her in a sex club with other men makes my skin itch.

"Yes, I'll be there."

We say goodnight and head home, the quiet in the car makes it feel like the air is humming around us. Neither of us is willing to end the peace with a discussion that I know in my gut will be painful for us both.

Walking through the door behind Audrey, I can't help admiring how fucking beautiful she is. Her long neck, elegant and regal, and that body. God, her body is sinful.

"I'm going to head to bed." Her gaze finds mine as she rolls her lips, uncertainty making her nervous. "Should I wait for you, or are you going to stay up?"

"

Moving to her, I cup her neck and she shivers as her head falls back. "Wait for me."

"Okay."

Her answer is soft, but the way she does as I ask, without fighting me, is all the indication I need that talking tonight isn't what we need. We need to reconnect. That bond we've been building needs strengthening before we talk.

Seeing Mrs. Price home, I go around the house locking up and making sure my family is secure. The two most important people in my life live here and it's my job to protect them.

When I slip into the bedroom, Audrey is sitting on the edge of the bed in a dove grey satin nightgown. The moonlight casts a blue light over her skin and hair, giving her an ethereal glow. Her head lifts as I enter, and it's impossible to look at her and not want her. I've spent the last ten years in purgatory. Wanting her and not being allowed to touch her and now she's mine. For now at least.

My cock is thick and heavy in my pants as I see her watching me walk toward her. I stand right in front of her as she looks up, a thousand thoughts running over her expression. I run my thumb over her lower lip and her eyes close with a breathy sigh that has my cock dying to escape its confines. "What do you need, baby?"

Her tongue flicks out over the tip of my thumb before I push the digit past her lips, and she sucks.

Fuck.

Her tongue curling and stroking, mimicking what she'd do to my cock. She's fucking beautiful, strong, and confident, but willing to show me this vulnerable side of herself. After everything I've done and put her through, she still lets me have this. It's a gift I'll handle with care. Pulling my thumb out, I wait patiently for her answer to my question, but she seems lost in thought.

"Tell me what you need, Audrey."

Her chin lifts, the arrogant tilt something I'm familiar with these last few years.

"I want you to fuck me like you hate me."

I don't know why she needs this, and it's impossible to fuck this woman like I hate her when I adore her, but if she needs that, I can give it to her.

My hand thrusts out fast, grasping her hair and tugging her head back. "You want my anger, my little slut?"

Audrey's eyes fall shut and a shudder wracks her body. Her nipples are hard peaks against the satin of her nightdress, begging for my touch.

"Answer me."

"Yes."

I release her, pushing her slightly away like I'm furious with her and part of this role bleeds into my emotions. I *am* angry but not just with Audrey for holding me at arm's length all these years, but also with myself for the mistakes I've made.

"Undress me, little slut."

I watch her closely for her reaction, never wanting to do something that will upset her in any way, but she squirms, rubbing her thighs together and I'd bet my house she's soaked.

Her hands reach for my zipper as I shrug my vest and shirt off, letting them land discarded on the floor. I hiss as her fingers run over my dick as she pushes my pants and boxers to my thighs.

Reaching forward, I rub my thumb over her hard nipple. "So pretty."

Then I grip the lace edges of the gown that barely covers her and shred it down the middle.

Audrey's gasp gives me a second to admire her as I step back and kick my pants and boxers free. She looks wild, her hair a delicious mess from my hands, the satin torn down the middle exposing her gorgeous tits, nipples pink, and begging for my mouth.

"Are you wet, Audrey?"

"Yes."

"Show me."

I stroke my cock slowly, trying to garner some relief but only my dick buried in her sweet cunt will give me what I need.

Audrey spreads her legs and leans back on her elbows, exposing her soaked pussy to my hungry gaze.

"Turn around and get on your hands and knees. I want to see what's mine."

She does as I ask, and I move in behind her, smoothing the fabric up over her ass, and exposing her cunt. My hands find her hips and I explore the softness of her skin before I drop to my knees and bury my head in her sweet cunt. I lick and suck, giving her exactly what she needs, her moans and whimpers driving my need higher. Her hips are thrusting back against my face, and I grip them and hold her still as I feast until she cries out, her climax dripping down my chin.

Licking my lips, I stand and pull her upright, her back to my chest and I take her chin, turning her into my kiss. There's nothing gentle about this. It's a battle of who will consume who first. Passion and things left unsaid are released as I kiss and bite before she yanks her head from mine. Her stunning brown eyes are filled with hunger and anger.

"Fuck me, Hudson."

Pushing her down so her torso is flat, I lift her hips and line my straining cock up with her tight, wet heat, before slamming into her. Her head falls forward on a groan and my fingers tighten on her hips until I know she'll be sporting bruises in the morning, and I fuck her.

The rein on my control, that's normally leashed so tight, is straining, pulling at the frayed strands as I fuck into her. Nothing has ever felt so good and I know it never will.

"This what you wanted, Audrey? My cock buried in your cunt?"

"Harder."

God, this woman is going to be the death of me, and I couldn't fucking care less.

I fist my hand in her hair and lift her head to give myself more leverage and then I let myself go, knowing she can take whatever I give her. She was made for me.

The Enemy

Her pussy ripples around me and I can feel her climax coming, her body just on the edge. I need her to come because I won't last much longer. Sweat is pouring down my chest as my cock glides in and out to the hilt, giving and taking at the same time. Bending slightly, I find a deeper angle and she screams my name as her orgasm takes her under.

I turn her toward me, capturing her lips in my kiss to silence her as her pussy squeezes so hard I swear I might black out from pleasure.

As her body goes limp, I release her and force her to lean back against my chest, her head resting on my neck as I palm her delicious tits, teasing and toying. My spine begins to tingle as my climax barrels toward me and I bellow out a groan as my body shudders and I empty myself into her, spent.

Audrey's arm comes up and she pulls my head down for a kiss that is lazy and sweet.

Lifting my head, I find her gaze. "Did I hurt you?"

"No, that was perfect."

"Feel better now?"

She nods but doesn't elaborate.

Withdrawing, I lift her into my arms, her head resting on my shoulder, and carry her into the bathroom. I set her on her feet and strip the destroyed nightgown from her body.

"I liked that nightgown."

I look up as I turn the dial on the shower and warm, rainfall spray hits my skin. "I'll buy you ten more."

Audrey laughs, a sexy husky sound that shouldn't have my dick twitching so soon after such an explosive climax but does.

"Don't worry about it. I prefer your shirts anyway."

I nuzzle her neck as we stand letting the warm water soak us. "I prefer you naked."

"I noticed."

Taking the shower gel, I lather my hands and smooth over every inch of her skin. Cleaning her off and taking extra care to make sure her breasts and pussy are clean, making her come again as I do. The sounds she makes for me are like my favorite symphony. She returns the favor, laving my dick with her tongue, and making my legs almost give out as she steals another climax from me.

Once we're done, I wrap her in a warm towel and carry her to our bed. Setting her down in the center and drying her hair with a towel before blowing it with a dryer. I know she hates to sleep with it wet.

Once she's cuddled up against me, her head on my chest, I hold her tight not knowing if I should broach the subject of her pregnancy and miscarriage or if I should let her. So, I tell her that. Miscommunication got us into this mess in the first place. "Audrey. I'm not sure what do to from here."

She tenses and tries to pull away, so I hold her closer. Her default is to run these days, but it wasn't always like that. At least not with me, and I need that back. "Don't run from me. What I mean is, do you want me to bring it up or do you want to when you're ready? I don't want to fuck this up and hurt you more than I already have."

"Oh."

She's silent for so long afterward that I think she's fallen asleep.

"Thank you, Hudson. I spent so long thinking of you as my enemy, that it's hard to make the transition into whatever this is now."

I know what this is for me, but she isn't ready to hear it. She might never be, and I have to face that too. "I was never your enemy, Aud."

"I know that now."

She goes silent and then her body goes slack, her breathing evening out, and she sleeps in my arms. But sleep doesn't come easy for me, as I re-live every word she said to me tonight with the flashbacks of our past. Regret is a useless emotion, and not one I usually allow myself, but tonight it's riding me hard.

17. Audrey

I WAKE UP WRAPPED IN HIS ARMS, HUDSON'S SOFT BREATHS tickling my hair. My body has a delicious ache that only comes after a night of wild sex. The sound of his heart beating against my ear is calming and steady. An anchor in an otherwise turbulent world. The thought brings me back to his words from the night before.

How losing a parent feels like losing an anchor. I know that feeling in some ways because that's what it felt like to lose him all those years ago. I was adrift, and from that storm and the subsequent trauma, I built myself into this version of myself the world sees.

A confident, successful woman, who dominates in a man's world, but that wasn't always me. When I was young, I wore my heart on my sleeve. I explored new things with excitement and the freedom only known by someone who'd never suffered heartbreak.

Our years in Italy and Europe, when my father practiced law before returning us to the US to chase his dream to become a judge, had been happy. I'd learned to dance, to ride a bike, trust my body and mind because I had no reason not to.

Then I'd met Hudson and my heart had been consumed by him. I loved him with everything I had. He saw me for me, and not my name or my bank balance. He loved unreservedly, or so I'd thought. But looking back, he was holding back, not trusting me, like I had him. What had I done to warrant that mistrust? Was it my fault he hadn't confided in me?

"I can hear your brain whirring."

I smile against his chest before dropping a kiss over his heart. His husky voice sends a warm tingle through my body and it would be so easy to use sex to avoid painful conversations, but I'm not some meek girl who buries her head in the sand. I'm Audrey motherfucking Kennedy, or rather Carmichael, and I *will* face this.

"I was thinking about what you said last night about my dad being my anchor."

I feel his lips on my hair, his arm tightening around me. He doesn't even realize it, but even now he's doing that very thing.

"You'll get through it."

"I know." And I will, as much as the thought of losing my father carves me up, I'll survive it.

"The thing is, he isn't my only anchor. You are, too. Whether it's loving you, like I did when we were young, or hating you for the last ten years, you've always been there. A solid presence in my life."

"And now?"

Hudson's voice is gravel and silk as his chest rumbles beneath me.

"Now, I don't know what you are, but you aren't my enemy. What we have is so complex. It's friendship and intimacy, a partnership in this crazy scheme."

"I like that."

I take a deep breath as the clock clicks over to show six am on the dial. "Hudson, I want to tell you everything if you'll let me."

His arm releases me, and I fear he's going to walk away, unable to face all my baggage, but he doesn't. He rolls to his side so he's facing me and takes my hands in his, bringing them to his lips.

"You can tell me anything."

"When you left, I was heartbroken. I couldn't reach you on the phone, you stopped coming to school, and your dorm was cleared by the next day. I tried to stay positive but when my period was late, I was terrified and alone and angry and I still knew I'd forgive you anything if you just came back."

"Fuck, Aud, I'm so sorry."

"No. Let me get this out."

His nod is all I get, and I know from the set of his shoulders that he's finding this hard. "When I did the test, and it came back positive, I was scared but also so happy. I loved you and the thought of having a mini version of you in my life made me fall in love with my little bean."

"Bean?"

"I figured it was that size."

"Oh, okay."

"So, I knew that no matter what happened, I was keeping our child. I wanted you to know, and I think a part of me thought it would bring you back to me. So, I got Ryker to hack your school records and he gave me the address."

"That sneaky bastard."

A huff of a laugh escapes me at his words and I know he's trying to make this easier by lightening the mood. "I came looking and you were just getting out of a car outside your apartment. I was so happy to see you, and then you opened the door and unclipped a tiny baby from a baby seat. I watched you lift her into your arms like she was the most precious thing in the world. I knew immediately that you loved her, that she was the reason you left. Then your mom got out, but I only saw the back of her and she sure as hell didn't look like my mom. I saw you wrap her in your arms and kiss her head. And I thought you'd cheated. That you'd hidden this entire other family from me."

"I'd never do that to you, Audrey."

I press my finger to his lips and he kisses the tip. "I know that now, but at the time, I didn't. You had shared nothing about your family or situation with me, so what else was I to think? I left, got in my car, and I was crying so hard I could hardly see straight. It was raining hard and, between my tears and the rain, it was impossible to see the road."

I can still smell the pineapple-scented car air freshener I had hanging from the rear-view mirror. I still can't stand the scent to this day.

"Please don't say it."

I can see the plea in his eyes. He has the prettiest eyes, and they're filled with grief as he watches me. "I hit a tree. Not hard, but I hit my head and got slammed around. When someone came to help, I was dazed, and I asked them to call Lincoln. He met me at the hospital, and I was already bleeding. I knew I was losing our baby and all I wanted was you. I needed your arms around me. But then as the days and weeks went on, I got so fucking angry."

Hudson reaches up and swipes the tear from my cheek. "Baby."

"It was easier to hate than to feel the pain of my loss. I molded and shaped you into the villain and focused everything I had on hating you. Every move I made was to show you who I was and could be. Every decision I made, you were in the back of my mind, driving me. I thought it was hate but I know now it was grief and trauma. After a year, my periods had hardly come back and weren't the same."

I blush talking about this with him, even after what we've done, and he tangles his legs with mine to press closer. "They did some investigations and found I had Asherman's Syndrome. It's when scar tissue forms inside the uterus or, in my case, the cervix. It makes it almost impossible to have children. I was told my chances were nigh on non-existent. It was like a kick in the teeth. I'd lost our baby and now I was being robbed of my future family and I thought you were playing happy families."

His hand strokes my cheek as I cry. "I'm so sorry. If I could go back and change things, I'd do so in a heartbeat. The thought of a child with you is all I ever wanted and, because of my callous, reckless actions, I took it away from you."

The Enemy

"This isn't your fault, Hudson. This could have happened no matter what we did. Perhaps this is just my journey."

"I can see why you hated me."

"At the time, it was what kept me going. I would lie awake and imagine you with your family. How you'd be as a father and it tortured me because I knew you'd be amazing, and I was right. You're an amazing parent to Tia."

"Where did you think my child had gone or did you know about Tia before I introduced you?"

My fingers skim the stubble on his chin. "I thought you'd split up and she'd left with the child. And that made me angrier, that you had everything I wanted and had walked away. Not a word or sniff about the child ever came up in the media."

"You didn't ask Ryker to look?"

I shake my head. "No, a part of me didn't want the truth."

His hand cups my cheek and he bends his forehead to rest it against mine. "I need you to know, I'd never abandon a child of mine."

"I know that now. Honestly, I think I always knew that."

"I'm sorry I wasn't there when you needed me." He rolls to his back and takes me into the cradle of his arm. A loud sigh leaves him, and I know he'll need time to process this. He lost something too. He just didn't know it at the time.

"I guess I know why Lincoln hates my guts."

"He doesn't hate you."

A snort leaves him.

"Okay, maybe a tiny bit, but that's because he was there. He picked me up and put me back on my feet and has been with me every step. He's more than my cousin, he's the brother I never had."

"Do your parents know any of this?"

I shake my head, my hair catching on the stubble of his chin. "No, I never told them and, as I'd turned eighteen, the hospital didn't inform them. Linc handled everything."

Hudson goes quiet on me, and I sit up. He has one hand behind his head, causing his bicep to flex, the sheet pulled low exposing his ripped abs and the delicious V of muscle leading toward his cock. His eyes are on the ceiling, and I wonder if he can't face looking at me, now he knows I'm broken.

"I'm gonna take a shower."

He nods absently, and a sliver of disappointment fills me that he doesn't try and coax me into staying in bed with him. I guess I always knew this would end, but now it feels like it's over before we had a chance to begin.

I shower and wash my hair, rinsing the soap from my body. I gasp when the shower door opens and Hudson steps inside. He takes me in his arms and kisses me, but not like he usually does. Not with hunger or desperation, but with so much tenderness my heart flails in my chest.

He kisses me until I'm dizzy with it, my body yearning for something only he can give me. He lifts me and my legs wrap around him as my back hits the tile.

"I need you, Belle."

"You have me."

A shudder runs through him at my words but before I can say more, he's pressing into me. My body ceding to his hardness as he rocks into me, long and slow. His hands move over every inch of me until I'm nothing but putty in his arms. He whispers words I can't hear, and dots kisses all over my skin as water falls on us.

As I feel my body pulse with my climax, just out of reach, his hand moves between us and he circles my clit with his thumb, always giving me what I need. I cry out as my legs spasm, a wave of pleasure dragging me under as my orgasm pulses and my pussy clamps around his dick.

"Fuck, Audrey."

I feel him swell and fill me with his seed and it's a connection like none we've shared before. As if all of the obstacles between us have been swept away, leaving a clean slate.

"Can we get past this, Belle? Can you ever forgive me?"

The Enemy

His dick is still inside me, his arms holding me close as he breathes the question against my lips.

"I've already forgiven you, Hudson. We both made mistakes. But I don't know if I'll ever trust anyone again, and you deserve more than a woman who can't trust what is right in front of her. I just don't see how we can move forward with so much to face. I need to be there for my father and my mom. You have Tia and we're different people now."

"Are we? I still love you, Audrey. I always have."

His words rip a hole right through my heart, and I know I can't deny I feel the same, but I can't say it back, not like that.

"Hudson, a part of me will always love you, but we're not the same. I run a billion-dollar company and my days are filled with work."

"They don't have to be."

"Hudson, you don't get it. I can't be what you need."

"What is it you think I need?"

"A family. A wife who can give you children."

He shakes his head. "You're wrong. I need the woman I love fighting every battle we face beside me. I need you, not the promise of a family that may or may not happen anyway."

I shake my head as I disentangle myself from his arms and step from the shower. Grabbing a towel, I dry off as he follows me, naked and confident in his own skin.

"You think that now but, believe me, you'll change your mind when the shine has worn off."

He dries his chest with a towel, and I can't help but admire him. He's so handsome it should be a crime.

"Hey, my eyes are up here."

My head snaps up and I grin at his teasing even in the middle of such a serious discussion. He always had that ability to lighten any moment for me. His arms come around me and he pins me with his gaze.

"Audrey, if the shine hasn't worn off after ten years of you hating me, do you honestly think it will when I have you in my bed every night?"

"Maybe it's the thrill of the chase?"

"Do you honestly believe that?"

I shrug instead of answering because I know, for me, it won't but then he's whole, he's perfect in every way.

"You don't and neither do I. How about this? We spend the next however long living as if this is real. You give me a chance to show you what you mean to me. You give me the chance to win back your trust."

I know I shouldn't but the opportunity to pretend and live in this lie is too tempting. "And what do I get in return?"

I know what I'm getting, him making this whole ruse believable for my parents. He says he loves me, but he doesn't. It's just good sex for him. How can you love a broken doll?

"Orgasms, Audrey. You get as many as I can give you, and you get me, your husband, loving on you and betting on you every single day for as long as you let me."

God, when he says things like that, he makes me want to dive in with both feet and not worry about whether I sink or swim. He makes me want to believe this is real.

18. Audrey

"Hudson, you didn't need to drive us. I have my own car and driver." I glance across at Hudson, as we pull up to the bridal shop and he looks tense. I know letting go of any sort of control with Tia is hard for him, but he needs to learn.

"I don't mind driving my favorite girls around."

"And you're a control freak."

"Hey, I'm not a control freak. I just like to be in control."

I roll my lips so as not to let the grin I'm hiding free. "Okay, so just a freak."

He puts the car in park and unclips his belt. Hooking me around the neck, he pulls me to him, so my lips are teasing against his own.

"A freak in the bedroom, baby."

I smile. "Cheesy."

"I know, right? It's all I had."

"She'll be okay. I promise you."

He nods once and then kisses me hard and fast, pulling away before it can get out of hand, which our interaction regularly does. We can't seem to keep our hands off each other and, honestly, I'm not mad about it. Before Hudson came back into my life, sex was always perfunctory and done to fulfill a basic need. Now it's fun, and so fucking hot, it's like the chemistry between us is out of control.

My door is wrenched open and I jump.

"Okay love birds, enough smooching. We have dresses to buy."

I turn to Amelia, who is standing with Norrie, Lottie, and Eden. All wearing smirks on their faces.

"What's smooching?"

I turn to Tia, and Hudson glares at Amelia.

"Oops."

"I'll explain later. Go with Audrey and have a lovely time and if you need me, just call. I'll be around."

I get out and help Tia from her seat in the back before I lean into the car. "We won't need you. Go play golf or something."

"Actually, the boys are waiting for you back at my place. They thought you could all bond over some football game. Beck should have texted you?"

Hudson checks his phone and nods. "Yeah, okay."

I'd have to be blind to see how much he doesn't want to do that, but I'd love for him to have a better relationship with my oldest friends. "You should go."

A sigh that could bring down mountains leaves his chest. "Fine, but you owe me."

"Anything you want."

He gives me a look that would melt concrete, and I feel my entire body tingle from it.

"You're playing with fire, Belle."

"Aww, he calls you Belle. That's so cute."

Hudson doesn't take his eyes off me but responds to Eden. "She's always been my Belle."

"Okay, let's go before Romeo here seduces us all."

Hudson laughs and winks as I close the door. I sigh as Lottie loops one arm through mine, and I do the same with Tia.

"Let's go find you a dress."

"And me."

The Enemy

"Absolutely, sweetie."

We go into Dream Day Bridal and are met with a highly coiffed woman in her mid-fifties. Her smile is wide, and her eyes are seeing dollar signs. Wealth like mine could have made me an entitled asshole, but my parents would never allow it. I was always taught how fortunate I was and still am, and the value of money, so this could be interesting.

"Miss Kennedy, it's a pleasure to meet you."

"It's Mrs. Carmichael."

The woman blushes, but she knows this. It was on the booking, but people put so much stock in my last name it makes them act odd.

"Oh, I'm terribly sorry. It slipped my mind."

"Not to worry. These are my bridesmaids." I introduce her to Lottie, Eden, Amelia, and Norrie who have swiftly got her measure and are cool in their responses. I lay a protective arm around Tia, who is looking around the room with eyes full of wonder. "And this is Tia."

The woman looks at her with a face full of disapproval but offers me a polite nod with not an ounce of sincerity. "Oh."

"Oh?"

"Tia, why don't we go and look at the pretty dresses and you can tell us what you think Audrey might like."

Norrie puts her arm around Tia and leads her away with the other girls all chatting and treating her with all the love and respect I expected from them.

"I mean, this may be a little out of line, but is this really the place for her?"

My fists clench at my sides and I grind my teeth together to keep from blurting out all the vitriol I want to spew at this uneducated snob. With as much control as I can, I lift my head and look at the woman who has just lost what would possibly be her biggest commission of the year.

"It is out of line, it's rude, and passive-aggressive. People like you are everything that is wrong with the world."

"Well, I didn't mean anything by it. It was just an observation." She's flustered now, her neck stained and mottled red.

"Yes, you did. You just thought for some crazy moment you could get away with it. I have no idea what it is about my reputation that gives you that idea."

I hear the sound of the door behind me but don't take my eyes off Cruella, as I've christened her in my head.

"As I said, it wasn't meant to be rude."

"Is there a problem here?"

I cast my glance at a much younger woman who is dressed in jeans and a white t-shirt as she stands between us. She's stunning in a girl-next-door way, but I immediately feel a kinship with her, even as I bristle with anger. "And you are?"

"Shané Richards. I'm the owner."

Her smile is full of pride and warmth as she holds out her hand. I take it and pump it once. "Audrey Carmichael. Nice to meet you."

Her grin is genuine. "Oh, I know who you are, Mrs. Carmichael. I've followed your work for a while." Her cheeks are pink, but she holds my gaze, which I know isn't easy when I'm in a mood, and it earns my respect. "Not in like a stalker way, but you're an icon for women in business."

"Thank you. That's very kind of you to say."

"Can I help in any way?"

I glance at the assistant who has backed away and is now fussing with a veil a few feet away. "Your assistant was rude in her attitude toward my sister-in-law and presumed to tell me it wasn't the place for her."

I see her face turn from friendly to downright furious, her expression losing all humor or friendliness. "I am so sorry. That is not the ethos here. We welcome every single person through our doors." Her fingers twist and she looks uneasy like she wants to be honest but isn't sure if she should be. I would put her at around my age but there's an innocence about her still that I'd shed years ago.

"Can I be honest with you?"

"I'd prefer it," I say as my gaze flicks to Tia, to make sure she was okay.

"I didn't know you were coming in today. I think my soon-to-be former assistant kept it from me because she was expecting a big commission, and she hates that someone younger than her is running this place."

"Hmm." I hummed, respecting her honesty and deciding to give her the benefit of the doubt. "May I give you some advice?"

Shané beamed. "Yes, please."

I leaned closer and she mirrored me. "If you don't trust your staff, they shouldn't be your staff. Business is hard enough without fighting or distrusting the people who are meant to be in your corner."

"Agreed. She was kind of inherited."

I have no idea what the story is here, but I do know a genuine person when I see one. "Well, good luck, but I think it's best we leave."

Panic crossed Shané's features. "No, please. Give me another chance. I'll send Collette home and I'm happy to show you whatever you need, as long as you don't mind me in jeans."

"That sounds perfect."

I smile as I step around Shané, leaving her to deal with Collette, coming up behind Tia and Lottie who are looking at the prettiest cream bridesmaid's dress with sequins on the bodice.

"Find anything you like?"

Tia nods so hard, it's a wonder she doesn't give herself whiplash. "Yes, this one, and this one." Tia went on to show me every dress she liked, which was so far all of them.

"Well, you'll need to try them all on."

"Can I?"

Her eyes were luminous with joy, and it made my heart tug that I could do this for her. I hadn't realized how awful people could be until today. Or I had but I hadn't witnessed it. It hurt my heart to think Hudson had explained why he was the way he was with Tia.

"Of course."

Out of the corner of my eye, I caught Collette throwing her coat over her arm and slamming out of the shop in a huff.

Good riddance.

"Okay, are we ready to try some dresses on?" Shané stood with a tray full of Champagne glasses and one filled with juice and a cut strawberry on the side of each.

"Absolutely. Let the fun begin."

Norrie offered a toast and Tia clinked her glass, splashing juice over the side on the carpet. I tensed, waiting for a reaction, but none came, and I knew then that I'd help this woman succeed, and maybe a big fat sale would help.

Letting my friends choose a dress was hilarious as they were all so different. I dutifully tried them all on, but nothing was quite right, and I was beginning to lose hope that I'd find something. Even knowing this wasn't real, I still wanted to look beautiful for Hudson.

"I have an idea. Tia, can you help me?" Shané put her hand out for Tia who was beaming with all the attention she was getting. I nodded for Amelia to go too. As much as I liked this woman, I didn't know her enough to trust her with Tia, but I trusted Amelia with my life.

"I can't believe we all found our dresses." Norrie bounced her leg in excitement.

"I know, and you all look gorgeous." I drain the last of my second glass of Champagne.

"True but the real showstopper is Tia. I've never met a child with a bigger heart, and she looked so happy."

Pride fills my chest at Eden's words. "She looked beautiful, didn't she? And she has been so patient. Honestly, I love her so much."

Lottie squeezes my hand. "I can see why."

"I can't understand why Hudson never told anyone about her."

"I think he's just really protective of her privacy. He wants her to grow up surrounded by love, and the only way to ensure that is by controlling her environment."

"I get that, but for her to have a full life she needs to learn about the world around her and he needs to help her."

"I know, but it's not my place to tell him."

Norrie rolls her eyes. "Of course it is. Any idiot can see you two are in love, and if you want it to work, Tia will be a big part of that. You need a say, too."

Norrie is right, and I do want us to work out. Since everything came out, our relationship has gone from strength to strength. It's like we've slid into this perfect space and joined our lives seamlessly, but perhaps not all of the big things have been discussed.

Amelia and Tia walk from the back of the shop to the staging area where we're sitting on pale pink velvet couches. They're holding hands and grinning like two little kids with a secret.

Shané is a few steps behind them, and she's carrying a dress on a mannequin. As Amelia and Tia sit down beside each other, I get my first glimpse at the dress and my breath whooshes from my chest.

The gown is sexy and glamorous, a stunning sheath style, chic and minimalist with long sleeves, heavily embellished cuffs, and a gorgeous illusion back with a chapel train. The ivory coloring is perfect for my skin, and I feel my heart speed up with excitement.

"Oh, wow, that's stunning. Who is it by?" I finger the ivory silk as I admire the detail on the back.

"It's one of my own designs."

My gaze flies to Shané. "You made this?"

She nods with pride.

"It's truly spectacular. You're so talented."

"Would you like to try it on?"

"Yes."

Shané helps me into the dress as my friends wait and I can hear them all talking softly with Tia's voice just a fraction louder and full of joy.

When the last button is hooked, I stand and look and I know this is it. This is my dress.

"Would you like to try a veil before we show them?"

"Yes, please." I never thought I was the type of woman to want all the pomp that goes with a wedding, but being here now, I want it all. I was just missing the man I wanted to do it for.

Shané fits a veil to my hair and steps back. "Well, what do you think?"

"I love it."

Shané smiles clearly pleased with my reaction. "Let's go show everyone."

I nod and head back toward the sound of my friends laughing. As I enter, they all look up and the room goes silent. Lottie covers her lips with her fingers as she begins to blink furiously. Norrie gasps, and Eden and Amelia sigh. But it's Tia I'm watching as tears gather in my eyes.

Her gaze is full of wonder as she smiles widely.

"Well, what do you think?"

"You look like a real princess."

"Tia's right, you look beautiful."

I smile at Eden. "I feel like a real princess, but also like me, too."

"That's important. You need your dress to reflect you on the day. Your groom doesn't want to marry a stranger, and when you look back at these pictures in years to come, you want to know that you felt special all day."

"I love that. You have a true talent, Shané."

"Thank you."

"This is my dress."

Tia jumps up and races toward me and I hold my arms out as she hugs me tight.

"I love you, Audrey."

"Oh, sweetheart, I love you too."

I really do and it's dangerous and scary to love someone else when I don't even know if what Hudson and I have can last past the end date we set, but loving Tia wasn't a choice. Just like loving her brother wasn't.

19. Hudson

"Are you sure Tia will be okay all day?"

I grip my wife's hand and bring her palm to my lips. "Yes, she'll be fine. She was excited she got to help Mrs. Price pick out a dress for tomorrow."

Audrey shakes her head in wonder. "Can you believe we're getting married again in twenty-four hours?"

I can't, but I'm so incredibly happy about it, even if for Audrey it's all a ruse for her dying father. For me, it's as real as it gets. "I know, and this time we'll remember it."

Audrey laughs and it's light and airy. "I know and that's pretty important for a wedding. Can you remember anything from that night?"

I know now isn't the time to confess we didn't have sex and I have a thousand excuses ready for why I shouldn't, but I never want us to get derailed by secrets again, so I fess up. "If you're talking about our wedding night, nothing happened."

Audrey turns her knees toward me in the car and my gaze drops to the hint of creamy thigh in her short black sequin dress. By most standards it's modest but on her body, everything looks sexy.

"Hudson!"

I blink and snap out of the sexy fog she'd wrapped me in. "Sorry. You just look fucking gorgeous in that dress."

Her chin dips and she gives me a look with one brow raised, which I know is a warning or is meant to be, but fuck, she's hot.

"Hudson, I'm gonna need you to rewind and make that last comment compute for me."

Audrey rolls her hand in a rewind gesture, and I capture it in my hand and kiss her palm. "We didn't sleep together the night of our wedding."

Her eyes flare with annoyance and she tries to pull her hand away, but I don't let her, instead. dragging her closer. Her body language is closed but she lets me hold her and I take that as a win.

"I knew if you thought we hadn't had sex, you'd demand an annulment, and rightly so, but I needed more time with you. I needed more time to show you how much you mean to me and make this right."

Her hurt eyes lodge a stone in my chest.

"You lied to me."

"I did and I'm sorry. It was a dick move and I shouldn't have done it. But when I woke up and saw you lying beside me, your hair spread over the pillow like a fucking goddess, I knew I had to do everything I could to fix this between us. A divorce would give me more time, more opportunities."

"Do you realize how fucked up that is?"

Her voice is soft with none of the anger I expected. Burying my head in her neck, I kiss the pulse that beats wildly, and she shivers. "I'm sorry, truly I am."

"I forgive you, but don't pull a stunt like that again, Hudson. Trust is important and once it's gone, it's a hard thing to get back and we're still fragile. Don't break us before we have a chance."

Before tonight, I wasn't convinced that Audrey was all in with us trying for real, but that sentence cements it for me. She might not believe the wedding is real, but she believes in the relationship, and I won't give her another reason to doubt me.

"I promise. I love you, Audrey, and I'll prove to you that I'm a good bet."

Her lips find mine and we kiss. Tender and deep, it's the kind of slow languorous kiss that leaves you feeling drugged.

The car stops and I pull away. "We're here."

Audrey looks around as if surprised at her surroundings and I smile.

"Where is here?"

"Let's go find out."

"Hudson, you know I hate surprises."

Taking her hand, I help her out of the car. "You'll love this one. I promise."

"Fine, but if it's snake charming or anything involving rodents, then you're a dead man."

I chuckle as I pull her close. "What the hell goes on in that pretty little head of yours?"

"You don't want to know."

As we approach the door, the manager of the theater greets me.

"Mr. Carmichael, everything is set up exactly as you requested."

"Thank you." I shake his hand and he slips away as we enter the grand foyer of the building. Styled like the golden era of Hollywood glam, the ceiling is high with red carpets, gold chandeliers, and a wide curved staircase that takes us up to the private boxes.

"Hudson, what is all this?"

Audrey's head is tipped back as she takes in every detail with delight. I can't help but stare. She could have been the leading lady in a blockbuster and won the hearts of millions with her beauty. Instead, she's the leading lady in every dream I have. "Do you remember when we were young, we watched Moulin Rouge?"

Her head whips to mine and her grin is infectious. "Yes, and you said it was sappy."

I hook my arm around her waist and pull her close, my lips a breath away from hers. "I did say that. But, honestly, I wasn't watching the movie, I was watching you. Your reaction that day stayed with me even in my darkest days. I vowed to bring you to Paris to see it live, and while I can't do that right now, I thought we could have a private show here in New York."

Her eyes sparkle like diamonds with unshed tears. "Hudson, you didn't have to go to all this trouble."

"Nothing is too much trouble for you, Belle. If I could harness the moon and place it in your palm, I would."

Her hand strokes my cheek before she gives me a soft kiss. "Thank you. This means more to me than you can know."

"You're welcome."

I take her hand and we head up the stairs and into the private balcony. Champagne and strawberries dipped in chocolate are on a platter waiting for us. As I hand her a glass, I wonder if anything will ever be as perfect. "Here's to us."

Audrey clinks her glass against mine. "To us."

We watch the aerial dance and Audrey grips my hand, entranced with everything she sees, but like the time before, I can't take my eyes off her. She's stunning in her joy. There isn't a part of this woman that doesn't own me in every way. As it finishes, she glances at me for my reaction and I smile softly.

My body is humming with need for her, my cock in a near-constant state of arousal around her. She must recognize the hunger because her eyes turn molten.

"Take me home, Hudson."

"I thought I wasn't meant to see the bride the night before the wedding?" It's hard to believe we're getting married again tomorrow, only this will be with all our family and friends in attendance, which, on my side, is very small.

"I'm not the bride. I'm your wife."

God, I love that word. Who would have thought one word could hold so much power over me. "It would be my pleasure, wife."

That night as I undress my wife, I put every ounce of what I feel into her. As I devour her pussy with my tongue. As I toy with her nipples until she is crying out my name, I show her what she means to me, as her mouth moves over my cock, taking me deep until I groan in tortured delight. Until I settle my weight between her legs and slide my cock into her tight pussy as she whimpers for me.

We move like one body, her hips rising to meet each thrust of my cock. Her nails scrape over my back, scoring delicious lines of pain along my spine. I fuck her harder, deeper and she begs for more.

"Harder, more."

Lifting her so she straddles me, I look up into her feverish eyes. "Take what you need, wife."

Her hands move over her body, fingers toying with her breasts as I grip her hips and watch, mesmerized by the sight of her taking what she needs. Head thrown back in rapture as she works her pussy up and down my cock, riding me as we both hold on to our sanity by a thread. Nothing has ever felt as good as Audrey like this. Wild, free, confident, and all mine.

"I'm close, Hudson."

Moving my thumb, I stroke her clit in slow firm circles and it is all she needs, as her release clamps down on me. Her movements become erratic as she braces herself on my chest and takes and takes until she is limp.

Flipping her, I kiss her, as her fingers rake through my hair, scoring my scalp, and causing electricity to course straight to my cock. Burying my head in her neck, I thrust deep and hard, the sounds of her pleasure spurring me on until my own climax drags me under with a groan.

"Mine. You're mine, Audrey."

"Only yours, husband."

If I wasn't already wildly in love with her, I would have fallen in that moment. "I love you, wife."

She remains silent, kissing my neck and I pretend her not saying it back doesn't matter. We are in different places and Audrey is dealing with a lot. I know what she feels for me, she shows me with her body. I can wait for the words.

I make love to her until the early hours of the morning, watching as her lips fall open again and again in a wordless scream, her body holding me prisoner until I'm spent.

20. Audrey

Looking at myself in the mirror, it's like a surreal dream. This is my wedding day, and it feels nothing like I imagined it would. Not because I'm not crazy in love with my groom, because I am, and I'm not sure that's a smart thing. Hudson says he loves me, but if we hadn't got drunk in Vegas, we'd likely still be at odds. And if my father wasn't dying, this would've been over by now.

It all feels like we're building something on a foundation made of sand. Everything is finely balanced, and it makes my love for Hudson feel foolish. It's why I can't say it back. If I say it, it's real and that is terrifying.

"You look beautiful, Audrey."

I glance at my mom and Aunt Heather in the mirror. There have been a fair few tears this morning. The weight of why we're doing this so quickly is heavy in my heart. I'm going to lose my dad and I have no idea how to handle that. "Thank you, Mom."

I've styled my hair with an antique diamond comb that belonged to my grandmother. I have such wonderful memories of her. She was strong and loving and the one person who could keep my grandad in check. He loved her fiercely and, after she died, all his soft edges hardened. I never understood it until I lost Hudson, but I think I'm a lot like him.

"Is Tia okay?"

My mother gets a soft smile on her lips. She's really bonded with Tia. Almost as if she's a granddaughter instead of the sister of her son-in-law.

"She's fine. Norrie took her to see Hudson." She gets a weepy look in her eyes, which makes my nose sting. "He's such a good man for stepping up the way he did. Not many boys his age would've done the same."

"He loves her. She's his family. I don't think there was ever any question that he wouldn't look after her."

"As I say, you got yourself a good one, Audrey."

"I did."

A knock on my childhood bedroom door has me looking up to see my dad dressed in a black tuxedo. My gaze scans him, looking for signs that he's struggling, but he looks good today. The color that's usually missing is there and it gives him a more youthful appearance.

"Hey, Daddy."

"Princess, don't you look like a picture." He steps into the room as my mom grips his arm and kisses his cheek before giving a little wave.

"See you down there, sweetheart."

"Thanks, Mom."

My father steps into the room and moves toward me with such pride in his eyes my knees almost give out.

"Oh, sweetheart, you look beautiful. Hudson is a very lucky man."

"I'm the lucky one." Hudson is doing more for me than I ever could have expected from him, but my father doesn't know that.

"Not many people are lucky enough to find their soulmate once, but you two fought your way back to each other, through the hurt and the pain, and are stronger for it."

"Wait, what?" My father can't possibly be saying what I think he is, can he?

"What? You think I didn't know you were together in college?" His eyes twinkle with delight. "Sweetheart, do you honestly think I didn't keep an eye on you. Do you think I didn't know about the break-up and the accident afterward? I'm a judge. Nothing happens without me knowing. Although I will say I didn't know the details of the breakup until recently."

"Why did you never say anything?"

He grips my hands, and he feels strong and solid, my dependable father who will always be there. "Because, my sweet girl, it wasn't my place. My place is to guide you and be there when you fall, to offer my hand when you need it. If you wanted us to know, you would have told us. I trusted you to reach out."

"Are you mad?"

"Good God, no. You forged your own path on your own terms like I always knew you would. You found a man who loves you like you deserve to be loved. I'm so proud I could burst."

"Thank you, that means a lot. I only ever wanted to make you and Mom proud."

"Audrey, you did that the day you were born."

"Daddy, I don't want to lose you." Tears clogged my throat as I looked at the man who would be gone from my life soon.

"And I don't want to go, but sometimes we have no choice. But now I can go to my grave knowing that you're happy and settled with a man you love. You do love him, don't you, Audrey?"

He gave me a look I'd seen so many times before. It was his 'don't bullshit me' look, and I didn't have to, because I did love Hudson. "I love him so much it scares me."

"That's good. Love should be scary. If it's not, then you aren't putting your whole heart into it."

He kissed my cheek, and I inhaled the scent of his aftershave, the same one he'd worn since I was a child.

"I love you, Daddy."

"I love you, too. Now, enough morbid stuff, let's get you up that

165

aisle before your husband comes looking for you. He was pacing like a caged animal last I saw him."

I smile, imagining Hudson doing just that, especially as he asked Ryker to be his best man. I hadn't thought of it before, but he really gave up everything to raise his sister and become the successful man he is today.

"Let's do this."

I grip his arms as we descend the stairs in my family home where we decided to have the ceremony. It means my dad can grab a nap and rest when he needs to, and I have so many happy memories here. The formal living room has been cleared, and chairs, decked in silk covers, line either side.

An officiant is standing with his back to the fireplace and beside him is my handsome husband. Ryker taps his shoulder and he turns toward me. His eyes go bright as he rubs at the moisture in them with no care for who sees. Lottie will walk first, followed by Amelia and Norrie, and then Tia and Eden. Tia has taken a shine to Eden, and the feeling is mutual.

The music plays and I grip my father's arm as the whole world around me falls away. My sole focus is the man who is waiting for me with tears in his eyes. How has something that started off as fake become my entire reason for being?

As we reach the end, my father shakes Hudson's hand and kisses my cheek. "Be happy, sweetheart. Hudson, take care of my baby girl."

I don't tell him I can take care of myself.

"I will, sir." Hudson lifts his hand to my cheek and cups it as I lean into his touch. "You look absolutely breathtaking."

"You polish up pretty good yourself."

He's wearing a matching tuxedo to the groomsmen, but his buttonhole matches the red of my lips and the roses in my bouquet, which are calla lilies and ruby red roses that smell divine.

My hands shake and Hudson threads our fingers together, his solid presence anchoring me. The ceremony is a blur as we promise to love, to honor, and to be there in good times and bad. I want so badly for this to have been a choice we both made for us and not for anyone else. It feels so real, the emotion feels so real, and I can't separate fact from fiction anymore and I'm not sure I want to.

"You may kiss your bride."

Hudson cups both my cheeks in his hands and kisses me deep and long, making more promises between just us two. Shrieks and giggles break through our passionate kiss, and I pull back laughing against his lips as I wipe the smudge of my lipstick from him.

"We did it."

"Yes, we did, wife."

We agreed the photos would be natural candid shots of the day with just a few formal ones. It was best for my dad, and I didn't want to spend the time posing rather than enjoying every second and storing away every memory for when it was all I had left.

We opted for canapes and finger food, with a BBQ-style dinner later on. Everything is exactly how I would've dreamed my wedding would be. I never wanted too formal with hundreds of guests who only cared about our family name, not the people they were watching get married.

The board hadn't been especially happy, but Lincoln had explained the circumstances with my father and all of them had been understanding. Instead of gifts, we had donations made to a charity for blood cancers. I'd been hesitant as I didn't want this to all be about me, but Hudson had insisted.

"Can I have this dance?"

I grin up at Ryker. "Absolutely, but where is Eden?"

He smiles and lifts his chin toward the other side of the dance floor, where Eden is dancing with Eric and Tia.

"She's so great with Tia. She's going to be an amazing mom."

Ryker gets this soft look on his face as he nods. "She really will."

Ryker takes me in his arms and spins me around, making me laugh, before bringing me back into his hold. We've been friends so long, it's hard to remember my life without him. So, it's easy to read his look.

"Out with it, Ryker."

His boyish grin is infectious. "I never could hide anything from you."

"No, you couldn't."

"Are you happy, Aud?"

I pull back to look at him and cock my head. "Why are you asking me that?"

"Because I feel responsible. It was my wedding that started this."

I shake my head. "No, Hudson and I started long before, and you know it."

"I know that, but I feel like it came to a head in Vegas."

"It did, and while I wouldn't have chosen this, it is what it is. I'm making the best of a bad situation to make my father happy."

I feel a rush of air behind me and see Hudson walking towards Tia with his back to me. The scent of his aftershave makes my body hum with desire. I want to chase after him and make sure he didn't just hear half of our conversation, but Ryker has something to say, and I owe my best friend a few minutes.

"But do you love Hudson?"

"Yes, I do love him and it scares me stupid."

"Why? Because he looks at you like I look at Eden, and Beck looks at Amelia."

"You're worried about him."

"I'm worried about you both. I love you like a sister, Audrey, and I'd hate to see this end badly and, yes, for Hudson too. He's a good man, despite what has happened in the past."

"I know and I'm doing my best to navigate this situation as best I can."

"But you love him, and he loves you."

"I love him, and he says he loves me, but it wasn't enough last time. Sometimes you need more than love. He wants children and I can't give him that."

Ryker shakes his head. "No, you don't, and there are ways to make a family that doesn't involve you setting fire to his favorite bar."

The Enemy

"What in God's name are you talking about?"

"Your, you know, downstairs area is his favorite bar."

"Oh my God, how do we own a sex club together when you can't even say the word pussy?"

"I was being respectful to your new title."

"Don't be a doofus, Ryker."

"Fine, but my statement still stands."

I'm not sure he's right but as the day goes on and my friends and family laugh and celebrate our marriage, I wonder if maybe it's enough.

Arms come around me from behind, and I sink into his hold, with a sigh.

Hudson kisses my neck, his palm on the flat of my belly. "I missed you."

"I missed you too, husband."

"Ready to get out of here and make this official this time?"

I turn in his arms and run my palms up his chest. He looks at me like I'm everything he ever wanted. "Take me to bed, husband."

With a growl, Hudson kisses me hungrily, his teeth sinking into my bottom lip. "The things I'm going to do to you tonight, Audrey Carmichael."

"Is that a promise?"

"It's my solemn vow, wife."

21. Hudson

HEARING AUDREY SAY SHE WOULDN'T HAVE CHOSEN US AND that by being with me she's making the most of a bad situation for her father has thrown me. Today has felt like a new beginning for us, or for me at least, but for Audrey, it's about fulfilling the dying wishes of her father.

I'd been about to cut in with her and Ryker when I heard the comment and walked right past instead. My head is a jumbled mess as I accept handshakes and congratulations from everyone. I found Tia with Eden and my sister threw herself into my arms, declaring it the best day ever.

Her utter joy and delight over every little thing pulled me from my funk, but it hasn't dimmed the hurt. I'm madly, hopelessly in love with my wife, and I have no idea how she really feels.

I know she enjoys being with me, and that the sex is off the charts. She isn't faking that; nobody is that good an actor. Can that chemistry be enough to make her see that what we have is real? I hope so because, at this point, it's all I have to offer her.

It always seems to come back to this. I'm not good enough for her, never have been, and despite my success, I'm still not. She's almost royalty in our circle, and I'm the poor kid who worked his fingers to the bone to have the glimmer of a chance with her.

Like a magnet, my gaze is pulled to her, and I stand and move toward her, wrapping my arms around her and kissing her neck. "I missed you."

Her body seems to melt into mine as she sighs. "I missed you too, husband."

That sounds good but is she saying it because she thinks I want to hear it? And, God, I want to. "Ready to get out of here and make this official this time?"

She turns in my arms and runs her palms up my chest, and my dick goes hard from just that touch. She looks at me like I'm everything she ever wanted, and I want to believe it so badly.

"Take me to bed, husband."

With a growl, I dip my head and kiss her like a starving man, sinking my teeth into her bottom lip. "The things I'm going to do to you tonight, Audrey Carmichael."

"Is that a promise?"

"It's my solemn vow, wife."

We make the rounds, saying goodbye and her father shakes my hand. "Look after her, son."

"I will, John." My heart feels heavy, knowing that he won't be with us for much longer. That Audrey is going to suffer with the grief that, while natural, is unimaginable unless you've been through it.

I say goodnight to Tia as Mrs. Price takes her back to her place for the night.

"Night, Huddy. Night, Belle."

Audrey crouches down and runs her hand over Tia's ivory flower girl dress, which has little red petals sewn into the hem. "Thank you for being the best flower girl ever."

"Really? You think I'm the best?"

"Absolutely."

My heart feels full watching them interact. Tia loves Audrey and I know the feeling is mutual. I'd been so worried about the shopping trip, but Tia had come home talking non-stop about how much she loved it and I have no doubt that was down to Audrey.

We check into the Madison Hotel bridal suite and I sweep her into my arms, carrying her over the threshold.

"Hudson."

"What? I want to do this right."

Audrey loops her arms around my neck and laughs as I carry her inside, kicking the door shut with my foot. I don't stop until we're in the bedroom and then I set her down gently on the bed. Tossing my jacket on the couch, I pour us both a glass of Champagne and hand her a glass.

"Thank you."

"To wedded bliss."

"To wedded bliss."

We clink and I take a sip of the smooth cool liquid. "Stand up, wife."

Audrey shivers and I know from her peaked nipples that it isn't from the cold. She does as I ask and stands, her hands down by her sides.

"Such a good girl."

I walk around her, and the air almost buzzes with anticipation as I loosen my cuffs and roll my sleeves up. "You look beautiful in this dress."

"Thank you."

"You'll look even more beautiful when I fuck you in it." I have a primal need to mark her, to watch my come seep into her skin until there's no doubt who she belongs to.

Audrey stays quiet, her brain switching off as she lets me control her pleasure. This is where I get the most trust from her. In the bedroom, she's wholly mine.

I make it to the front of her and sink to my knees so that I can worship her like the Queen she is. Lifting the lace of her dress to her thighs, I groan when I see the suspenders she's wearing.

"Is this for me?"

"Yes."

I hand the edges of her dress to Audrey to hold. "Lift it higher, show me that pretty pussy, wife." I know I'm being demanding and overusing the word 'wife', but it's like I need the reminder. It feeds a need in me.

Audrey lifts the dress and I shudder as I'm met with her bare pussy. No panties to hide how wet she is from my hungry gaze.

"Is that your way of saying you've been naked beneath this dress all day? That you let other men dance with you in their arms with your naked pussy hidden only by this scrap of silk?"

"Yes."

"I should punish you for teasing me."

"It's not a tease. I thought of you the whole time."

Her answer pleases me and my dick strains in my pants. "Did you now?"

I swipe the finger with my wedding band through the soaked lips of her pussy, gathering the wetness before sucking it into my mouth. I hum with pleasure at the taste of her need on my tongue and Audrey whimpers.

"You taste like perfection. You make me hungry, Belle. Do you want me to feast on you?"

"Yes. God, yes."

I waste no time burying my head between her thighs as I eat her cunt like it's my favorite meal and it is. Her hands fist in my hair as she tries to remain standing. I lick her from front to back, gathering her juices on my tongue and reveling in the fact it's me who does this to her and nobody else.

Flicking her clit with my tongue, I grip her ass as she tries to ride my face and hook her knee over my shoulder so I can get closer. Spearing my tongue through her folds, I fuck her with my tongue as her whimpers turn to loud moans.

"Oh, fuck. Yes."

Her dirty mouth makes my dick weep pre-cum.

"Do you deserve to come after teasing me, Audrey? After you told Ryker that we're in a bad situation. That you'd never choose me?"

I don't give her time to respond to the questions that spewed from me as if I had no control. I pull her clit into my mouth and suck as I spear her pussy with my fingers, fucking her and sucking until her legs give way and she screams her release, soaking my chin with her orgasm.

Before she can regain her feet, I stand and unzip my pants, releasing my aching dick. Spinning my wife around, I push her gently so she's bent over the bed. I flip her dress up over her back and thrust into her to the hilt, the force of it sending her forward, where she catches herself on the bed. I grip her hips and smooth my hands over the perfect skin of her ass, teasing the tight bud of her ass with my thumb.

"Gonna fuck you here."

My body is unleashed as I fuck her hard, taking my pain out on her, but she takes it and thrusts back into my cock, asking for more. Because she was made for me, and I just need to make her see it.

The thought steals the anger from me. I slow my driving hips, bending my knees so I hit that place inside her that makes her whimper.

"Oh yes, there. Don't stop."

I roll my body over her back and catch her ear lobe with my teeth. "I'll never stop, Audrey. Not wanting you or loving you, and if it's the last thing I ever do, I'll prove to you that we belong together."

"Yes."

Rolling my fingers over her clit, I tip her over the edge and she tightens like a vice around my cock as she comes. Her pussy fluttering around me is like pure heaven. Before she's even finished, I pull out and flip her around, shoving her dress up and laying her on the bed before I slam back into her. "Look at me."

Her hazy, sex-drugged eyes find mine and I could drown there.

"I want you to see who makes you feel like this. I want you to know it's me, Hudson Carmichael, your husband, who makes you come so hard your legs give way."

Her feverish gaze is full of desire. Sweat coats my skin and the smell of sex fills the room.

"Only you, Hudson."

Her voice is so full of sincerity that I want to believe her. I want to beg her to love me back like I love her, but I don't. I kiss her, winding my tongue along hers, tasting her desire as she arches against me.

"You're mine, Audrey," I growl my release into her neck as she holds on to me with all her limbs.

She's mine, and I'm hers. I know it, and before the night is over, so will she.

"Hudson."

I shake my head. "Forget I said anything."

"But I need you to know I didn't mean it how you took it."

"I said forget it. It's our wedding night. Let's enjoy it."

Audrey's gaze searches mine before she nods. "Okay."

I kiss her lips and stand, leaving her looking freshly fucked and beautiful.

"I'll order room service. You're going to need your energy for what I have planned."

Audrey grins sexily and my knees almost buckle. "Can't wait, husband."

22. Audrey

"Thanks for coming with me today, you didn't have to."

We're in my parents' living room, a week after our beautiful wedding and, as usual, Hudson is beside me. Tia is in the kitchen with my mom, plating some cookies and my dad has popped into the library to get a book on modern-day villains and what it means for the world, which he thinks Hudson will enjoy.

"It's fine. I told you, I like your parents and Tia loves your mom."

I smile, remembering the excitement on Tia's face when we said we were visiting. She'd been a little quiet this week and it's good to see her back to her old self.

"Here it is. I thought it was on the shelf, but it was on the coffee table stack."

I hustle to take the book from my dad, who is looking very pale today. He's also a little breathless and that concerns me. "You should have let me find it for you."

"I'm not a child who needs coddling, Audrey."

"I know that, but I love you and I want to help."

"You have helped. You help me every day by living your life to the fullest."

The Enemy

I hand the book off to Hudson, who gives me a wink, which makes all my insides go gooey.

"Here we go, finger sandwiches and cookies, made by Tia Carmichael," my mom says with a grin that I know is forced.

Tia smiles proudly as she carries the plate of cookies to the table and sets them down carefully.

"Well, young lady, what do we have here?"

Watching Tia with my dad makes my heart squeeze painfully. He would have been such an amazing grandfather. Now he'll never get the chance, even if I could provide him with grandkids.

I half listen as Tia animatedly tells my dad about the sandwiches, and he gives her every bit of his attention. That's what sticks in my mind about growing up. My parents were busy people, but when I had their attention, I had it fully. I didn't need to fight with a parent who had their head in their phone or their attention split. I see it with Hudson, too. When he's home, he gives us everything.

It's why I know that cheating him out of the chance to become a father is wrong and, although it breaks my heart, I don't see how we could work. I glance at him to find him watching me, his head cocked.

"You, okay?" he mouths and I nod, but he knows me too well. "Audrey, will you help me with something in the kitchen?"

I lift a brow at his not-so-subtle question. "What?"

Hudson scratches his cheek. "I wanted some ice and wasn't sure where it might be."

"For your coffee? You want ice for your coffee?" I'm teasing him now, and I can see my parents sniggering and Tia frowning.

"Maybe he wants Iced coffee. My teacher likes that, too."

Tia is so cute defending him.

Hudson points at his sister. "Yes, I fancied an Iced coffee."

"That seems odd. You usually hate cold drinks."

He shakes his head, and takes my hand, pulling me up with a deep chuckle that moves through me like a caress.

"For the love of God, woman. Can you just do as I ask for once in your life?"

He shoves me in front of him out of the living room, and I let a laugh fall from my lips.

Once inside the kitchen, he backs me up against the island, with his body. "You think you're funny, don't you?"

"I mean, I'm not Ellen funny, but I'm pretty funny."

"Yeah, you're cute, I'll give you that."

He kisses me, nipping my lip before stroking his tongue along mine. I sigh as the tension and worry in my body temporarily abate. Hudson grips my hips with his big hands, stroking his thumbs over my belly.

Pulling away, he looks at me with concern. "Talk to me."

I shrug, not wanting to say it out loud, but also knowing he's like a dog with a bone. It's what makes him so good at his job. "Watching my dad with Tia just got me. He won't ever have that. He won't ever get the joy of being a grandparent, of watching Lincoln's children grow up, and he'd just make the best grandpa ever. It's so unfair."

Hudson cups my cheek and tilts my chin so I have to look at him and let him see me laid bare and vulnerable again. His tongue swipes his lip and I just want to lose myself in him. Let him take it all away, but I know I can't always use him to fix things for me.

"Belle, I'm not going to lie to you and say it will be easy. Losing a parent is one of the hardest things you'll ever face. But it's going to happen, and it's fucking unfair, and cruel, but you'll get through it."

"I don't want to get through it. I just want it all to go away."

"Oh, Audrey, if I could, I'd take away all your pain, but I can't. Listen to me. Enjoy the time you have. Maybe consider taking some time off work so you can spend time with him. Say the things you need to say, make the memories that are being stolen while you can."

I shake my head. "I don't know if I can. We have so much going on with the new company."

"Fuck the new company. It will still be there when your father isn't. Nothing is more important than this. If you need me to speak to Lincoln, I will."

I stroke my hands over the soft cotton of his black t-shirt. It's a perfect fit, snug around his biceps and chest and loose around his hips, which means it lifts when he moves his arm up, giving me a glimpse of his gorgeous abs.

"I appreciate the offer, but I can handle Linc. Let me give it some thought over the next few days."

Hudson drops a quick firm kiss on my lips and frowns. "Now, where's the fucking ice?"

I laugh as I wrap my arms around his waist and he pulls me close, resting his head on mine, and pressing his lips to my hair.

"It's going to be alright, Audrey. It won't feel like it, but it will be."

The words 'I love you' are on the tip of my tongue. I can't deny them any longer, but giving in to the need to tell him how I feel serves nobody. It's selfish on my part and Hudson has given up enough. I won't allow him to give up the chance at a real family because of me and I know in my heart he'd choose me. I just can't let him.

A loud thunk from the other room, followed by a scream from Tia, has me pulling out of Hudson's arms and running like my life depends on it. When I make it into the living room entrance, I see my father collapsed on the ground. I rush to him and sink to my knees beside my mom.

Panic grips me so hard I can barely breathe, my brain a scrambled mess over the sight of my father looking pale and frail on the ground, blood coming from a cut on his brow.

"Daddy."

I turn him to his side as he groans and my mother cries and fusses.

"Mom, what happened?"

"He went to get up and just collapsed."

I feel a hand on my shoulder and look up to see Hudson with his arm around a terrified Tia. "I called an ambulance. Give me some room and let me check him over. I have my first aid certificate."

I move back reluctantly and Tia grabs my hand. I haul her close, holding on like she's my lifeline and my husband checks my father over.

"Looks like he fainted. His pulse is good, and he's breathing fine."

Moments later, the first responders arrive and check my father over. He's awake now and grumbling about everyone fussing. Saying he just stood up too fast and got dizzy. We all know that's just a symptom of his ever-deteriorating health.

To be safe, the paramedics decide to take him in and get him checked over by his oncologist. Dad agrees but I know it's only for our sake. He wants us to go home though and, after a slight argument, I agree but only if my mom promises to call me as soon as she has news. Suddenly everything is more real than ever, and time is slipping away like sand through a funnel.

As he's driven away with my mom beside him, Hudson wraps his arm around me. Bolstering me, holding me up, and I know what he said earlier is right. I need to make the memories while I can before it's too late.

"I'm going to take some time off."

His lips find my cheek. "I think that's a good idea."

Neither of us are saying it, but the end is looming like a gaping maw filled with darkness.

23. Audrey

"Hey, I need a favor, but you can say no."

I look up from the book I was trying to read on homeopathic healing as Hudson comes into the room, his hair a mess from where his hands have been running through it. He's usually so composed, so this must be serious.

Placing the book aside I stand. "Of course, anything. What's wrong?"

Hands on his hips, he looks irate as he paces in agitation. "You know I sometimes help women get out of difficult situations?"

He'd told me all about how he worked with the shady Lorenzo Abruzzo, head of the Italian Mafia here in New York. At first, I'd been horrified, but when he explained what they did, I understood it more. Hudson couldn't save his mom from the life they had or her subsequent death, but he could help others. It gave him a purpose outside of being a parent to Tia.

"Yes."

"Well, one of the women I've been trying to help has killed her abusive husband and I need to get to LA and help her."

"Oh no, that's awful."

"Yeah, it was. She's only twenty-two and he was forty-three. Usual story. He sold her the dream and then became her nightmare. We were hoping to get her out, but it seems she snapped the last time he hurt her and she stabbed him with a kitchen knife."

"Good for her." I fold my arms. "She should have cut his balls off for good measure."

Hudson snorts. "Remind me never to cross you."

"Like you'd be so stupid."

"So, I need you to watch Tia and pick her up from school. I should be home tomorrow. I wouldn't ask unless I was desperate, but Mrs. Price is sick with the flu."

"It's fine. I'm happy to help."

"Thank you." Hudson kisses me quickly and starts for the door. "I'll put you on the approved pick-up list with the school."

"No problem. Just help that girl. She doesn't deserve to go to prison for defending herself from a monster."

Hudson winks and sends me a smile. "Will do, Belle."

As the door closes, I get the feeling that I miss him already, which is completely insane considering his car is still in the drive. Shaking off the feeling, I head into the kitchen and look through the fridge to see what I can make for dinner. I'm not quite as gifted in that department as Hudson, but I can pull something together.

I see little inspiration and know some of that is down to my lack of appetite. The last two weeks and spending time with my dad every day has been wonderful. But it's also shown me just how sick he is, and he's fading fast. He gets tired quickly, he sleeps a lot, and his pain is an issue, even though he tries to hide it from me.

He said he was spending the day with Mom today as it's their wedding anniversary and likely the last. I blink rapidly to clear the sting of tears, but my nose is clogged with them. Everything is just too much. Being in the house isn't going to help, but I'm not fit for company either.

I decide Tia and I will get pizza for dinner. I slip on some flat shoes and grab my bag. There is a place Tia and Hudson love, and it will be a nice treat for her and me. I spend the day wandering around the shops, killing time, and getting a start on some holiday shopping. I pick up a pink ballerina doll that's wearing a tutu in pale pink. I know Tia will love it. She talks non-stop about dance lessons and, so far, Hudson has resisted. I get that he's worried for her safety, but he needs to relax and let her breathe, or he'll suffocate her. But how can I possibly tell him that? He's been with her since she was born, and I'm just coming into their lives now. What right do I have giving advice to a man who has given up so much for his family?

I feel the hair on my neck stand on end and turn to the window. I'm trying to be discreet, in jeans and a casual navy blazer, but as I stand in the toy store looking for a present for Tia, I catch a glimpse of one of the paparazzi who's particularly invasive on the other side of the street. He works for a rival company to my network, and I detest the man. He leaked the story about Beck, Amelia, and Xander and almost ruined them.

I place a call to my security and head out of the back of the shop to my car as I see Hank, my head of security, walk towards him with two other members of my protection team. Safely in my car, I head to the school, excited and nervous as I try and navigate the pick-up line without pissing off the seasoned moms. I'm aware from Lottie that there's a very certain etiquette for this kind of thing and, silly as it might seem, I don't want to get it wrong. Hudson is trusting me with this, and I don't want to let him down.

I needn't have worried, it all goes smoothly, and Tia runs to the car, and jumps in the back.

"Hey, Audrey. Where is Huddy?"

I glance in the back seat as she buckles herself, watching until she's all clicked in before I answer her and begin to drive off. "He had to go away for the night for work, but I thought we could hang out and get pizza."

I'm surprised by how nervous I am about her answer, but Tia is the easiest child I know.

"I love pizza."

I grin. "I know you do, sweetheart, so do I."

I drive us to Gianni's and park down the street before I help Tia from the car. Holding her hand, we walk the short distance to the pizza parlor. Hank and his team text to say the pap guy is dealt with and he is headed my way. I'd usually tell them to go home, but with Tia's safety at the forefront of my mind, I let it go. My team is discreet, and she won't even know they're there.

Hudson texts to say he had landed and was headed to the police station.

"Hey, Tia, let's take a selfie and send it to Huddy."

Tia wraps her arm around my neck, and I snap a quick pic and send it over. He gives it a heart to say he's seen it, and it makes me smile.

Our joined hands swinging between us, Tia and I chat about her day as we're seated in the cute little authentic Italian restaurant. We place our order, deciding to share a margarita pizza and leave some room for ice cream.

"So, tell me about your day. What did you do?"

"I was a star. Mrs. Greggs said I was the best and she wants me to play a star in the show this year."

"Wow, that's fantastic. Tell me all about the show?"

"It's about a little star that doesn't shine very bright, and all the other stars think she's broken, but then when Mr. Moon needs help, the little star is the only one who can help."

"That sounds beautiful. Would there be singing and dancing?"

Tia nods excitedly, and then gets quiet, a sad look falling over her pretty face.

"Hey, what's up?" I reach for her arm across the table.

"Huddy will probably say no."

God, she breaks my heart. "Hudson loves you so much. He just worries about you."

"I know, but I'd be a good star."

"You'd be a great star and maybe we can talk to him and see if we can persuade him."

The Enemy

Her features transform and I know for a fact, if it's in my power to do it, I'll make all this child's dreams come true.

"I love you, Audrey."

"I love you too, sweetheart."

"And I love Huddy, and Huddy loves you."

"I love him, too."

The pizza is delivered and Tia chatters excitedly about the show. I wipe the sauce from her face as she gets up and twirls around, showing me the spin she has to do.

"Careful, Tia."

I smile apologetically at the man at the next table who gives me a glare.

Fuck him.

"And then I have to jump." Tia climbs on her chair, and I stand, terrified she'll fall, but it's too late. A flash from outside blinds us both and before I can catch her, Tia is falling.

24. Hudson

By the time I come out of the interrogation room, it's clear to me that other forces are at play here. Lizza, the woman I'm defending is black and blue and still covered in blood, but the police are giving her zero consideration. It turns out her husband was a respected businessman with friends in high places.

It's why Lizza ended up reaching out to Lorenzo via the app we have requesting anonymous help. I've managed to get her a shower and a single cell for the night at least, and she's seen a doctor. But I might need some of Lorenzo's help with this one.

I check my phone and panic seizes my gut when I see I have eight missed calls from Audrey. I call her straight back and she picks up on the first ring.

"Hudson, thank God."

"What's wrong?" My first thought is her dad.

"It's Tia."

The bottom falls out of my world at those words. "What happened."

"We're at the hospital. She broke her arm and is in surgery."

"I'm on my way."

The Enemy

"I'm so sorry, Hudson."

Audrey is crying and the sound breaks me as my legs eat up the distance. "It will be alright. I'm heading to the airport now and will be on the first flight home."

"I have my private plane waiting on the tarmac for you."

Jesus, that must have taken some doing, but this is Audrey, and she cares for Tia. Thank you."

"Hudson, I really am sorry."

"Why are you sorry?"

An uncomfortable niggle starts in my gut and builds to a flutter in my chest as I think of what Tia must be going through, how scared she must be.

"There are pictures of her online. We went for pizza and they followed me."

Fucking hell. I grit my teeth in the hopes that I can tamp my anger down and not react. "I'm on my way, just don't leave her."

"I'd never leave her alone."

"I'll be home as soon as I can."

I hang up and race to the airport. Clicking through my phone, I see hundreds of images of Audrey and Tia. Walking along the street, arms swinging, looking happy. Tia and Audrey eating pizza at Gianni's, our favorite place, and a warm feeling soothes my anger at not being able to get to her sooner. Then a picture of Tia twirling around the restaurant and standing on a chair comes up before a series of images of her falling and Audrey rushing to her side. The bastards captured it all, the paramedics, the ambulance. Audrey's worried expression as she tries to soothe a crying Tia.

I have the urge to toss my phone but grip it tight instead, reading the headlines, each one more scandalous than the last. They're calling my sister my secret love child. Then the next says she's Audrey's daughter, but the heiress is so ashamed she hides her away.

I board the flight and barely acknowledge the flight attendant as she asks if I need anything.

"No, just get us in the air."

The whole flight, I tortured myself with the lies and vitriol the rag that spilled Xander Reynolds' secrets to the world has spouted. Each one is more disgusting than the last. My sweet sister has become the subject of a social media frenzy, and all because Audrey didn't listen.

She should've been more careful. She should've just gone home. Instead, she has exposed my sister to this vile online abuse.

I'm out of my seat before the plane comes to a stop and waiting impatiently for the flight crew to open the doors. I brush past them, not caring who I offend as I race down the steps and thank God find a car waiting for me. Ryker is inside, which I wasn't expecting.

"Why are you here?"

His blond brow shoots up at my aggression. "Hopefully to stop you from going off the deep end."

"What the fuck does that mean?"

"Audrey is upset, and I don't want you making it worse."

I bristle at Ryker poking his nose in where it isn't needed. "My wife is my concern, not yours."

"I know, but I also know how protective you are of Tia."

"She's my fucking sister, man. Do you have any idea how many times we nearly lost her when she was little? I sat by her bed more times than I could count watching her breathe because I was worried if I closed my eyes she'd stop."

"I get that."

"No, you don't. None of you have any fucking clue. She's every-thing to me. She got hurt because I wasn't there for her and my wife didn't listen."

The car pulls up at the hospital and I jump out before Ryker can stop me. I race to the elevator but it's five floors up. I head for the stairs instead and take the steps two at a time. I burst on to the pedi-atric floor and come face to face with Beck. He works here as a cardiac surgeon and is one of the best in the world, so it makes sense, but my brain doesn't consider he might be here for Audrey, it goes straight into Defcon 1. "Is Tia's heart alright?"

The Enemy

I get right up in his face, my chest heaving from trying to force the anger and panic into a box and failing at both.

"Relax, Tia is fine. Her heart was never an issue. She had a bad break but it's all fixed and she's in recovery."

It's like letting the air out of a balloon as the adrenaline and fear have no place to go. "Where is she?"

"Through that door. Audrey is with her."

I push past him and take a deep breath to calm myself as I shove against the door. I expect to find Tia looking small and frightened, but what I find is her whispering softly with Audrey. For a second, I allow myself to watch them, to imagine what it would be like to have them both in my life forever. But it's a fool's errand. Audrey is never going to trust me again. She can't even admit she loves me, and I know she does.

If we don't have that, what do we have? Good sex and a one-sided infatuation. I need to start protecting myself and my sister from the inevitable pain of her leaving.

"Hey, munchkin."

Tia looks up and her eyes are slightly glassy from the drugs, but she looks happy enough. Audrey, on the other hand, looks wrecked. Her eyes are red, her skin pale, and her hands shake as she straightens Tia's sheet.

"Huddy."

I move to Tia and take the other side of the bed to Audrey. Placing my hand on Tia's soft hair, I kiss her temple, breathing in her scent and thanking God that it was nothing more serious. This is bad enough, not to mention the shitshow in the media.

"What you been up to?"

"I broke my arm, and Audrey got me pizza, and I'm going to be a star."

"Busy day, hey?" I stroke my finger over the pink cast on her arm, a shudder moving through me at her tiny bones breaking. It makes me want to hunt down the pap responsible and tear him limb from limb.

"Yeah, I'm tired."

"I know, sweetie, why don't you sleep?"

"Will you and Audrey stay?"

I look at Audrey and she returns my stare with a slight nod.

"Of course. I'm not going anywhere." But I know Audrey will be and it's time to redraw some boundaries. I let myself get carried away with this whole fake marriage and ended up believing it could be real because I've loved her for so long. I'll always love her, but Tia needs me, and I can't let distractions like being head over heels for my wife tear me from her well-being.

"Can we talk?" Her voice is almost apologetic.

"Sure, outside." I nod to the corridor now that Tia is snoring softly.

Audrey rubs her hands on her thighs with nerves and I resist the instinct to reassure her. I need to do this.

"I'm sorry."

I close my eyes and push out a breath through my nose. "What were you thinking?"

"I thought she'd enjoy it."

"No, Audrey, you didn't think. You just did what you wanted like you always do."

"That's not fair. That child needs a life. She needs to spread her wings and learn that the world around her isn't this terrifying place you seem to think it is."

I begin to pace, feeling anger rippling up my spine. "Are you fucking kidding me right now?" I point at Tia's room. "She's in that bed with a fucking broken arm because the world is exactly as bad as I say it is. The whole world is talking about her like she isn't human. Like she's a juicy story for them."

"I know and I'm very sorry, but not everyone is like that."

"And not every person is a serial killer, but you wouldn't walk through the park at night on your own, would you?"

She's silent and I think my point is landing.

"You're trying to protect her but you're going to harm her if you don't loosen your grip, Hudson."

The Enemy

"Don't tell me how to raise my sister. I've been with her every single day, and you have no idea what you're talking about. You waltz into her life and think you have a say, and you don't."

I hear the sharply indrawn breath and hate myself for hurting her. "Look, Audrey. I don't mean to be a dick, but the truth is, we took this fake marriage shit too far. We, or perhaps I, got lost in the dream that it could be real, but it can't. You'll leave and I have to pick up the pieces. I think it best if we go back to just friends."

"Friends! You want to forget everything and be friends? We were never friends, Hudson, so how the hell can we go back to something that never existed?"

"Roommates then. I can't keep doing this with you when I get nothing back. You're one foot out the door all the time. You always have been."

"Excuse me, it was you who ghosted me."

I pin her with a look, which must betray my exhaustion. "And you're never going to forgive me for it."

"I already forgave you." Her lip wobbles but she seems to pull a shield of strength around herself. I can see her walls going up around her heart.

"No, you didn't, or you would've trusted what we had and admitted you loved me, too. Instead, you made excuses and kept me at arm's length."

"Trust goes both ways, Hudson. You want me but you don't trust me either or you wouldn't be blaming me for what happened to Tia."

"I'm not blaming you, Audrey."

"Yes, you are and you're right. I'm no good at this. Maybe it's just as well I can't have kids. I'd be a shit mother."

"You'd be an excellent mother but to do it, you have to be open to getting hurt. Even now you can't say it, can you?"

Audrey clamps her lips shut and I sigh, my head hanging to my chin. "Just go home, Audrey. We can talk tomorrow when I'm less of a mess over Tia."

A hiccup slips from her lips but as I reach for her, my ability to hold her at arm's length when she's hurting vanishing, she runs away.

"Audrey."

Her hair billows out behind her as she runs and I let her go, because what can I say? We might love each other but it wasn't enough the first time, and it isn't enough this time either.

25. Audrey

I SHOVE MY BASICS INTO A BAG AS TEARS FALL ANGRILY DOWN MY cheeks. Guilt over what happened to Tia is like a knife in my chest. The way she cried for Hudson, the pain etched on her gorgeous face, and my utter despair that this was all my fault.

I knew Hudson would be angry, but I never anticipated he'd react with such coldness. I'd wanted so badly for him to wrap me in his arms and hold me and tell me it would be okay. When he'd walked into the hospital room and barely looked at me, my heart had sunk, and nausea had swirled in my belly with dread.

I take one more look around the room we've shared and a sob erupts like lava of emotion. He'd made me believe that he'd always be there for me, he'd made me think I could trust him. Yet the first sign of trouble, and he'd walked away, just like last time.

Grabbing the t-shirt he wore yesterday from the hamper, I toss it in my bag like some junkie needing one last fix, and I walk out of the room, out of his home, leaving my key on the table by the door.

I ask my driver to take me to my apartment and close the barrier between us so I can wallow in private. My phone rings in my hand

and I jump as I see his name on the screen. Everything in me wants to hear his voice, but I have to protect myself. I can't allow him or me the luxury of a long-drawn-out goodbye. This entire thing was a mistake to begin with. I should have just been honest with my parents from the beginning.

Fresh tears fall as the call cuts off and I think of my parents. They'll be devastated when they find out, but what choice do I have?

Arriving at my apartment, I walk inside, and I'm struck by how cold and stark it is compared with the home I'd shared with Hudson and Tia. I'd thought it was classy but all the white, black, and gold lacks the beautiful chaos I've grown to love.

I don't want paintings by some million-dollar artist, I want pink and green splotches on printer paper that are meant to be flowers. I want dolls strewn about the place and the beads from a charm bracelet underfoot.

I take a shower and let the tears that just seem endless purge from my soul in the hope that it will allow me to feel better. When it doesn't, I decide I need action. Dressing in my comfiest leggings and an old hoodie of Hudson's because I'm a glutton for punishment now, I make a call.

"Hey, how is Tia?"

"Hey, Linc, she's doing okay. Hudson is with her now."

"What's going on? You sound upset."

"Hudson and I ended things."

"You what?"

"It's for the best."

"Wait, I'm putting you on speaker. I'm with Beck and Harrison."

I sigh, knowing it's pointless to argue and maybe this is for the best. I can tell them all at once and be done with it.

"Are you okay, Aud?"

"Yeah, Beck, I'm fine."

"You don't sound fine," Harrison argues, never one to take things at face value.

The Enemy

"You know what, I'm not fine. The man I love has ended our fake marriage, my father is dying, and I've never felt so lost in my life."

"He's a dead man."

I shake my head at my hot-headed cousin's threat. "No, he isn't. Just leave it alone."

"You love him?" Beck is always the one who picks up the things I try to hide.

"Yes, but it isn't enough."

"You want us to come over?" Harrison is shuffling around in the background, and I can imagine him dropping everything to come over and console me. All of them would and it's why I love them all so much.

I shake my head, even though they can't see me. "No. I called because I need a favor from you, Linc, and it's a big one."

"Anything."

I close my eyes as a fresh wave of tears prick my lids, but these are in relief and gratitude. "I want Kennedy to buy Redman Media."

"Isn't that the media outlet that broke the story about Beck, Xand, and Amelia?"

"Yes, it fucking is," Beck hisses, anger at the way the people he loves were treated still evident in his tone.

"Yes, and it was one of their reporters who followed me yesterday and is now writing all this bullshit about Tia and Hudson. I won't allow them to hurt that child or Hudson."

"What will you do with it?"

"Fire every last one of those assholes and clean house." My blood is humming with the need to fix this, and this is the only way I can. I haven't had the heart to read what's being written but, from Hudson's reaction, it must be bad.

"I'm in if you need an investor," Beck says like spending millions on a news outlet just to close it down is normal.

"The shareholders will take some convincing, but if they say no, I'm happy to go in personally."

"Me too," Harrison adds. "And I'm certain Ryker would too. They gave him a pretty rough time about the sexual harassment case."

"Are you sure? This is a lot of money."

"They hurt you and the people you love. If this is what you need, Audrey, then this is what we do."

"I don't deserve you guys."

"Of course you do. Now, do you want me to make some calls, or do you want to handle it?"

"Let me."

"You want us to come over and help you get drunk and bad mouth Hudson after, or shall we send the girls?"

"You don't need to do that."

Beck groans. "We know that. We want to make sure you're okay, and this is our way. We missed too much when you were hurting last time, and we won't make the same mistake this time. You're one of us, Audrey, and we stick together."

"But less hairy and better looking, right?" I ask, wanting to break the intensity.

"Less hairy for sure. Better looking? I'm not sure Norrie would agree."

I laugh. "Oh, she'd definitely agree with me."

Harrison chuckles. "Probably right."

I say goodbye and promise to call them when the ball is rolling and then get to work. By the time I'm finished with Redman, they'll wish they'd never heard my name. I work flat out all afternoon and into the evening, making deals, pulling together the funding, and calling in every favor I'm owed until I have everything for a hostile takeover of the Redman Media Group.

Then I call my friends to come over, because I know being on my own isn't what I need right now. I glance at my phone and the ten missed calls from Hudson and my heart aches. Then I see he's sent me a text notification. My finger hovers over the delete button, but I can't bring myself, to press it. What if something has happened to Tia? I'd never forgive myself. I guess that's how Hudson feels. I can't even be angry about his reaction, because, in a lot of ways, I understand it.

But I'm devastated with what we said afterward, how he accused me of being half out the door and not forgiving him. How he ran again and told me to go home. That's what hurts. That's what makes me feel so twisted up inside.

Opening the text on a blown-out breath, I read.

HUDSON: AUDREY, PLEASE PICK UP.

HUDSON: I'M SORRY FOR YELLING AT YOU. I WAS JUST SO WORRIED ABOUT TIA.

HUDSON: SHE'D BEEN ASKING FOR YOU. I TOLD HER YOU WENT HOME TO SHOWER.

HUDSON: WHY THE FUCK IS YOUR HOUSE KEY HERE???

HUDSON: YOU LEFT!!!

HUDSON: AUDREY, PICK UP THE FUCKING PHONE.

HUDSON: PLEASE TALK TO ME.

HUDSON: FINE, I'LL GIVE YOU SOME SPACE, BUT THIS ISN'T OVER. WE NEED TO TALK LIKE ADULTS. I NEVER SHOULD HAVE SAID THOSE THINGS TO YOU.

I place the phone face down and pour myself a neat whiskey. My hand shakes as I take the first sip and let the burn warm me. I know he regrets what was said. Hudson is a good man, but he can't take back the words. Our first sign of trouble and he pushed me away. How can I trust him with my heart when he doesn't trust me with his? And even if we could work that out, there's still the issue of my infertility. That isn't going anywhere and one day he could decide he wants kids more than me and then where would I be?

The buzzer goes and I move to the door to find the whole gang on my doorstep, even baby Isaac.

"Wow, I didn't expect you all."

Norrie kisses my cheek and hugs me tight, before pulling back to look at me. "You okay?"

I nod, worried if I speak, I'll collapse into sobs of despair.

"You're not, but you will be. We're going to get you through this, Audrey, and for the record, you're way hotter than Harrison."

"Hey!" He comes up behind her and swats her ass.

"Oh calm down. You know I think you're the sexiest man on the planet."

I laugh at their antics as I'm enveloped in hug after hug from my friends. Each one of them bolstering my bruised heart. But even as we spend the night laughing and getting drunk, with a hefty helping of my tears thrown in for good measure, I know it's not the same.

I love these people, but Hudson is my soulmate. He's the person who I thought got me in a way nobody else ever did.

"So, he just told you to go home?"

Amelia is weaving slightly, her words slurred as she sits between Beck and Xander.

"Okay, you've had enough, Wildcat."

Xander takes her drink, and she frowns. "Hey, you're not the boss of me."

Xander smirks. "No, but he is."

His eyes flit to Beck who smirks and finishes the rest of Amelia's drink. God, they're so hot together. I'm not into sharing but if anyone could tempt me it would be the heat between those three.

"Yep, told me to go home, after saying I hadn't forgiven him because I couldn't even say I loved him." I huff and knock back my drink.

"Wait. You never told him?" Lottie and Eden are the only sober ones in the room, apart from Isaac, who is asleep in my spare room.

"Nope."

Ryker cocks his head as he strokes Eden's thigh. "Did he say it?"

I nod, my eyes closing, my brain a foggy mess of emotion I'm scrambling to put into order. "Yep." I pop the P on the word and try and focus. This isn't the best way to drink a twenty-year-old McCallan whiskey but whatever. It's getting the job done and numbing me from the pain of losing him. I hiccup a sob and Xander puts his arm around me as Eden reaches for my hand. I lean into his hold and close my eyes, pretending it's Hudson, but it's no use. Nobody feels like he does when he holds me. Like I'm the most beautiful precious thing in the world.

"Why didn't you tell him?" Lottie's voice is soft.

"Because the last time I did that he left me, and I was right. One little mistake and he pushed me away. Jerk."

"Yeah, jerk."

Lottie slaps Lincoln on the arm. "Stop that. Hudson is a good man, and he loves her."

"Funny way of showing it."

Harrison raises his glass to mine, and we clink, spilling liquid down the side and onto my thirty-thousand-dollar black rug.

"Oops."

"No, I agree with Lottie and you boys are hardly in a position to talk. Linc, you had a tantrum and took a woman back to your apartment. And, Harrison, you threw me out of the house and threatened to take Isaac away. And you, Xander. You ran so fast you put the Flash to shame."

"Hey, I fixed it and apologized." Harrison looks contrite and I snigger.

"Yes, you did, and I'm sure when Hudson pulls his head from his ass, he will too."

"He already did, via text."

"See, he fucked up, but he loves her, and I don't think you guys realize how hard this tight-knit group is to break into. Hudson wasn't born with a silver spoon. He fought for it."

"So did I," Harrison defends himself.

Norrie kisses his cheek. "I know, babe, but you didn't do it looking after a sick mother and a newborn with multiple health issues."

My friends know everything about that now and about my fertility issues and miscarriage. It's cathartic to have no secrets.

"What are you saying, Norrie?" I ask as I try and make my eyes decide which one of the two of her is speaking.

"That you need to talk and be honest with each other about what you feel and what you need, and do it when tempers aren't frayed or emotions are overwrought."

"Fine, I'll speak to him tomorrow."

Eventually, my friends leave, and I fall into bed. Knowing tomorrow is going to be hard, I drink three glasses of water and take some Tylenol before I go to bed. Today has been rough, maybe tomorrow will be better.

A WEEK HAS PASSED SINCE I LAST SPOKE TO HUDSON, AND MY heart is breaking in two. I miss every part of him and the life we were building, my limbs ache from not being able to touch him. Yet I still can't make myself answer his calls. I know I'm a coward, that I should speak to him, but all I'll allow myself is to read his daily updates on Tia.

God, I miss that child. She became ingrained in my heart so quickly, and now there isn't only one but two gaping holes where she and Hudson have permanent homes. I've buried myself in purchasing Redman Media and spending every moment I can with my parents. I still haven't told them about Hudson and me, as my father seems to grow frailer with each day I spend with him.

I tell them Hudson is with Tia and they understand but I see the way my mom watches me carefully as if I might splinter at any moment and it breaks my heart that I'm adding to her worries.

I keep telling myself every day that tomorrow will be better, that I survived losing him before and I will again, but this is different. I told him he was my anchor, and he let me go. No, he pushed me away. I might never have told him I loved him, but he knew. No, this is for the best. He was right about one thing. We got carried away and this is the right thing for us both. A clean break.

I'm getting ready to go over to my parent's house when I get a call.

"Hey, Mom, I was just about to head over. Do you need me to bring anything?"

The Enemy

My gut bottoms out at her next words.

"Audrey, you need to come to the hospital straight away. It's your dad. It's time."

No!

I'm not ready, I'll never be ready, and the only person I want to hold me as the phone slips from my hand isn't here—again.

26. Hudson

"When is Audrey coming home?"

Tia asks for the hundredth time today, her voice has the whiny tone that only children can achieve, and it grates on my heartstrings. "I'm not sure."

The truth is, I'm starting to think she won't.

When I lost my temper and reacted by pushing her away instead of holding her closer, I made the second biggest mistake of my life. The first was letting her go in the first place. Before she'd even left the hospital, I knew I'd made a horrible mistake in letting my own fears and anxiety control my emotions. I said things out of fear and guilt for leaving them alone to get ambushed by that reporter. I should've been here instead of trying to save some woman I barely knew.

"I miss her."

Tia's lip wobbles and I hug her close. "Me too, munchkin."

"Then why isn't she here? She promised she'd help me be a star."

Tia has told me all about her school production and how her teacher wants her to play the lead. My instinctive reaction was to say no, but Audrey was right. I need to let my sister breathe and grow if she's to have the life she deserves.

The Enemy

I'd gone online as I sat beside Tia's bedside and watched her sleep and the positivity towards Tia and the support for her had been over-whelming. Thousands of people had headed to social media to berate the newspaper who'd leaked the pictures and the subsequent bullshit stories.

So many people with Downs themselves were telling their own stories and it had made me see what Audrey was saying all along. Tia isn't a secret to be hidden, she's a beautiful, wonderful child who should be celebrated. I thought I was protecting her, but I was, in fact, harming her. She's now signed up for the school play and additional dance classes. The fear will always be there and the need to protect her will never leave but that's okay too.

"I can help you be a star."

Tia's lip pushes into a pout. "It's not the same."

"I know."

I think the time has come for me to get our girl back. I've given her time to nurse her wounds but it's time we sorted our differences out once and for all. I can't go on feeling like half my soul is missing without trying to fix this.

I'm heading to the kitchen when I get a call from Lincoln Cold-well. I haven't heard from him since Audrey and I argued but I've been expecting this call. "Coldwell."

"Carmichael. Get your ass over to the hospital and support my cousin like you promised."

My heart takes off at a gallop as I grab my keys. "What happened?"

"Her father is dying. He has hours."

"I'm on my way."

"And Hudson, you can thank Lottie. If it had been up to me, I wouldn't have called. You broke your promise to be there for her when she needed you—again."

He hangs up and I stare at the screen, regret and self-recrimina-tion battering me hard. But overriding that is the need to get to her. I jump into action and call Mrs. Price, and she agrees to let me drop Tia with her on my way.

I get to the hospital and race to the floor where I find all of her friends waiting. Lincoln looks up before going back to ignoring me. Ryker approaches and he looks solemn, the mood evident of what's happening behind the closed door of the room at the end.

"How is he?"

Ryker shakes his head. "Not good. They don't think it will be long."

Nausea ripples up my throat and I'd give anything to save her from this. From watching the person she loves so much take their last breath.

"Is she with him?"

Ryker nods. "Yeah, her and her mom are with him."

"I didn't know it had gotten so bad."

"Yeah, he was brought in yesterday morning and she and Ruth haven't left his side."

"Yesterday? Why didn't she call me?"

"You told her to leave, Hudson."

"No, I told her to go home, to our home, and we could talk later. We were just throwing crap at each other, so I figured it was best if she left and we cooled down. I never expected her to leave."

"Well, she thought you were rejecting her again, that you wanted her gone. Why would she think that?"

I shake my head and let my head hand low. "I told her we should pull back and put our relationship back to friends only."

"What the fuck? Why would you say that?"

"Because I'm an asshole who panicked instead of using his brain."

"Well, you fucked it big time. I'm not sure she's going to forgive you this time. She's a mess."

"I know, but I have to try. I love her."

"Then you better come sit."

Ryker clamps a hand over my shoulder, and I move to sit beside him and Eden near the door. The mood is solemn, but I get a soft smile from Norrie and a chin lift from Xander. The silence is oppressive and heavy with grief. Behind that door, the woman I love is saying goodbye to her father. Watching his chest rise and fall, waiting for the moment when the next one doesn't come. When all the words not said will stay unsaid. When the world becomes a little bit darker for his absence.

"You know she bought Redman Media and fired every reporter they had on staff. She did that for you because she loves you. She may not have said it, but she showed up. You might have said the words, but you didn't show up."

"Lincoln, that's enough."

I glare at Lincoln, as his angry gaze holds mine despite his wife's rebuke. "No, Lottie, he's right. I didn't know she'd done that, but I shouldn't be surprised. She always takes care of those she loves. Like making sure Lottie was okay after you fucked up, and giving Norrie a place to stay after Harrison threw her out of their home, or putting herself in danger to get Noah Cabot in a place we could take him down. She cares for everyone and yet none of you noticed how broken she was inside."

I stand and pace, brushing my hair back in frustration. "I fucked up, okay? I was a dick, and I should have been with her when the call came, but I'm telling each and every one of you right now, I'm here for the long haul. I love her and I'm going to prove I'm worthy of her and that I'm not leaving her ever again and if any of you get in my way, I'll take you down."

"About damn time."

Lincoln smirks and we share a look, as if he finally believes me. I nod and sit, my leg bouncing with the need to be in there with her and shielding her from the pain.

An hour later the door opens and Audrey steps out, her sobs wracking her fragile frame. "He's gone."

Her watery eyes find mine as I stand and move toward her and she falls into my arms, her head hitting my chest as the pain erupts in a torrent of ugly tears. I stand silently holding her, my arms encasing her in all the love I feel for her.

I murmur gentle words of reassurance and do everything I can to take away her pain, even knowing that nothing but time will do that and then not completely. Around me, Lincoln and Heather are consoling Ruth, but I only care about Audrey.

"Why are you here?"

I dip my lips to her cheek to hear her mumbled words easier and so she hears my answer. "I told you I would be."

"But you hate me."

"I could never hate you. I love you."

She only cries harder then, and I hold on a little tighter. Eventually, her sobs turn to sniffles, and she pulls away, my shirt soaked from her grief. Her eyes are swollen and red, and she looks like a broken doll. "I need to go."

"Let me come with you. Let me be there for you, Audrey."

She shakes her head as I feel her pulling away from me, mentally and physically. "No, I need to be with my mom and Tia needs you."

"You need me."

She shakes her head sadly. "I needed you. I don't need you now."

Her words are flat and without any emotion and I know this is the pain and shock talking. "You don't mean that."

"I do. Draw up the papers, Hudson. We're done."

Audrey stands and walks toward her mother, her shoulders sagging under the weight of her loss.

"I'm not giving up, Audrey. You're my wife and I love you."

"Do you? Because when you love someone, you don't run or push them away when they make an innocent mistake."

"I messed up."

"We both did, Hudson."

She gives me a wan smile and I feel my heart crack, but it's quickly filled with a jolt of determination. She's hurting and bruised from our fight and now she feels like I've let her down again, and I have, but it ends now. I'm going to prove to her how much I love and adore her if it takes the rest of my life.

THAT NIGHT I HAVE MRS. PRICE KEEP TIA, EXPLAINING WHAT has happened and I sit in my car outside Audrey's parents' house. I see the curtain of her childhood bedroom twitch and her silhouette in the window. I know she sees me and that's okay. I need her to know that even if she won't see me, I'm here and I'm not leaving.

The next four days are spent in my car with brief visits home to see Tia. Eden has kindly offered to spend time with her, and I've learned to gratefully accept help instead of trying to do everything myself.

On the fourth day, Audrey comes out.

I roll the window down and she walks across the road, her arms folded. She looks fragile but so fucking beautiful it takes my breath away.

"You need to go."

I shake my head. "I told you. I'm not leaving."

"Why are you doing this?"

"I told you. I love you and you're my wife."

"That wasn't real, Hudson."

I glance at the wedding band on her finger and then at the one on mine. "It was to me. It was the most real thing in my life, and I'm not giving it up."

"I could call the police."

"Oh, please, we both know you won't." Audrey goes silent but doesn't leave and I take it as a good sign. "How is your mom?"

Audrey shrugs, causing her sweater to fall off her shoulders.

God, I miss her.

"Okay, as well as we can expect."

"What about you?"

"I feel numb."

I nod, knowing she'll move through the stages of grief in her own time and that it isn't a linear process like people think it is.

"When is the funeral?"

"The day after tomorrow."

"I'll be there."

"I don't need you."

"You've never needed me, Audrey. I need you. I always have."

"I can't do this."

She turns and walks away, and I have to curb every impulse not to leap from the car and race after her. To beg on my hands and knees for her to forgive me, but I know she needs to work this through, and I'll wait while she does.

27. Audrey

"Here, Mom, drink some tea."

My mom waves my hand away and turns toward the window. "I don't want tea."

"You have to have something. The car will be here soon."

My mother turns glossy eyes on me and my heart breaks at the pain I see.

"I don't want it."

I place the teacup on the side and sigh. "I'm only trying to help." I sink into the chair at the kitchen table, every bone in my body feeling like lead. God, this is so much harder than I thought.

"You should let him come in."

"Who?"

She glances back out of the window, and I follow her gaze. Hudson is in his car, dressed in a black suit, waiting for what I'm not sure. He's hardly left and my ability to keep him from breaking down my walls is almost non-existent.

"Your husband."

"Mom."

"Oh, I know. It was all pretend in the beginning, but it's not now, is it?"

My head snaps up to see her watching me. "You knew?"

"We both did. But we also knew the love between you was real. Am I wrong?"

I shake my head. "No, but it's complicated."

My mom grips my hands in her freezing cold ones and I cling to her. "No, sweetheart, it's not. You love each other and, yes, mistakes have been made but nothing that can't be fixed."

I know in my heart that the words we exchanged can be overcome and that we could work it out, but it doesn't change all our issues. "Mom, I can't have kids."

"I know."

"You do?"

"Yes. I found a leaflet on Asherman's Syndrome in your room."

"Why didn't you say anything?"

"Because it was up to you when you told us that. What happened?"

I spill all of it, on the day we laid my father to rest, I unload all my emotional garbage onto my mother and watch her come alive again.

"I'm so sorry, darling. I wish we could have helped you. I feel like we failed you."

"No, Mom. No. You and Dad are," I clear my throat as the tense of my dad being alive and in the past clogs my airways, "were the best parents I could have asked for. I just didn't want to face it. Discussing it was real and I didn't want to face it."

"Does Hudson know?"

"He does now."

She cocks her head as if trying to understand. "And that changed things for him?"

"No, he says he loves me and that it doesn't matter to him."

"So, what's the problem?"

"Mom, you've seen him with Tia. He was born to be a father. I can't rob him of that."

The Enemy

"He's already a father. She may not be his daughter, but he's done the job of a father for the last ten years. How are you robbing him?"

I pause trying to figure that out and realize I'm not. "I'm not, I guess."

"So, who are you to decide what he wants? Would you allow him to do the same thing to you?"

"He did do the same when he ghosted me rather than give me the choice to stand by him and Tia."

"And how do you feel about that?"

"Angry. He had no right to make decisions for me."

My mom raises one brow and all of a sudden it all makes sense. I'm doing exactly what he did to me, and I hated it. "What if he changes his mind down the road, Mom? He was so angry when Tia got hurt and we said some awful things to each other."

"Sweetheart, when you were five, your father lost you in the supermarket. I was so furious I threatened to divorce him if he ever took his eyes off you again."

"Really?"

She gets this soft smile on her lips. "Absolutely. And when you were seven, you fell out of that tree and broke your arm, and your father told me he was hiring twenty-four-hour security to watch you because I couldn't."

"Wow, I was a handful."

"You were but my point is, parenting is the most terrifying thing you'll ever do and Hudson has been alone for ten years. Letting someone in and sitting back a little will be hard for him. You'll have countless fights over things like that and say things you don't mean and will regret but love will always be the glue. You just have to communicate."

"Thank you, Mom. That makes sense."

"Well, your father and I didn't raise a fool."

I hug her tight, inhaling the familiar comforting scent of Chanel No 5 and then we head out to give my father the sendoff he deserves. I drive with my mom and Aunt Heather but I know Hudson is close behind us and it gives me strength. I feel his eyes on me as I get out of the car and hold onto my mother's hand.

He nods and gives me a look so full of longing that I can't keep the walls up any longer. I hold out my hand and he steps up and slides his palm across mine and everything feels less daunting.

"I've got you."

The service is beautiful and I cry my way through my eulogy until Hudson steps up and takes over delivering it with a deep resonance that makes me cry harder. He stands behind me at the graveside, one arm around me, the other around my mother, holding us steadfast, and taking the weight of our grief as his own.

All day he acts as a buffer without my asking and demands nothing in return. He makes sure we eat, that we drink, and that when things get too rough, we have a moment to ourselves. Eventually, when the last person has left the house and only my Aunt Heather is left, we get a minute to ourselves.

"Thank you for today."

He cups my cheek and I feel my body unfurl with the hint of desire. "I told you. I'm not going anywhere."

"I know but thank you anyway."

"You're welcome."

"How is Tia?"

"Good, but she misses you."

"I miss her, too." I don't know how to do this.

"I should go." Hudson turns to the door.

"Wait."

He turns to me with hope in his eyes and I realize how short life is. He could be taken from me tomorrow and I'd be left with nothing but regrets for what we lost. I won't dishonor my father's memory by living like that. "I want to come home."

"You want a lift to your apartment?"

I can see the hope warring with his need not to jump to conclusions. I step forward and lace my hands on his chest and feel him so warm and vibrant beneath my fingertips. His heart beating with life. "No, I want to come home to you and Tia."

Hudson's eyes close and he stifles a grin. When his eyes open, they're full of love for me. "Really?"

"Yes. Take me home, husband."

28. Hudson

I call Mrs. Price on our way home and ask her if she would have Tia overnight. It might be selfish, but I need this time with Audrey on our own. She's had an awful, emotionally draining day and I just want to hold her in my arms and reassure myself this is real, without the worry of whether my sister is okay.

Walking into the house behind my wife, I watch her stop in the kitchen and just take a moment to look around her. Sliding my arm around her waist, I pull her back against me and she leans into giving me her weight.

"You doing okay?"

"Yes. I just missed this place. My apartment stopped being my home when I moved in here." Her hand strokes my arm before she turns into my chest. "I guess I thought I'd never see it again, so I'm taking a second to drink it all in."

My fingers thread through her dark hair and she tips her head to look at me. She looks tired but beautiful, alive and in my arms, and I know there won't ever be a time I won't be grateful for that. "Life is short. I learned that when I lost my mom."

The Enemy

"It is and I'm going to live every second of mine from here on out and cherish those I love, starting right here in this house."

"I love you so damn much, Audrey Carmichael."

"I love you, too. Now take me to bed and prove it."

I take a second to really look at her, trying to determine if this is really what she wants, but all I see is molten desire and love for me.

"My pleasure."

I hoist her into my arms and carry her to our room, which is just as she left it. I haven't had the heart to move a single thing. It was easier to believe she was coming home if I left her stuff lying around.

"All my stuff is here."

I shrug, a little sheepish as I set her down on the bed. "It felt like you were just out of town for work if I left it. I couldn't face the thought that I'd never see you in here again."

"Hudson," her voice is soft as she tugs on my tie and pulls me down for a kiss.

I brace myself on the bed with one hand as her soft lips open, allowing me to taste her. Swirling my tongue along hers, I deepen the kiss as her hands begin to tear at the buttons on my shirt. Her fingers are urgent, almost frantic.

I pull away and yank at the buttons and tie as she attacks my zipper. A frenzied need to be inside her ignites in me, my blood humming with the desire to feel her tight pussy clench around me.

"Get naked, Belle. I can't wait."

Audrey fiddles with the side zip on her dress and I swat her hands away to help her. Soon I have her naked before me and we each take a second to admire the other before we're a tangle of limbs.

Hands roaming overheated skin, lips caressing and tongues tasting. There's no skill here, only the wild need to reaffirm our love, our connection.

I settle between her legs, my arms braced on either side of her head as her fingers run over the muscles in my back.

"You're so beautiful."

"So are you."

I chuckle at that. "Beautiful?"

"Men can be beautiful."

"If you say so."

I stop any retort as I pull her nipple between my lips, flicking the tight bud with my tongue. My cock is pressed up against her soaked pussy and I stroke my hips forward, sliding my dick through her folds until my crown hits her clit. A whimper tears from her throat and she arches against me, her hips moving as she tries to get closer.

She feels like heaven beneath me. My cock is pulsing as my spine tingles and I have to recite the constitution to stop myself from going off like a rocket and ending this before it begins.

"Hudson, I can't wait. Please?"

I can't deny this woman a thing, so I slide my palms under her ass, lifting her hips, and thrust deep. Her moan is half pleasure, half pain, and her body squeezes me so tight I almost black out. Nails score my skin and her cunt flutters around me.

"So good."

She stole my words, not that there are words to describe how good it feels to be inside her again. I thought I'd lost this and I'll never take it or her for granted. My thrusts become harder as Audrey moans and writhes in my arms. I kiss every inch of her as my thumb finds her clit and I stroke firm circles as she clenches and cries out her release. I try to hold on but it feels too good and, before I can stop it, my climax drags me under so hard everything goes black for just a second.

Our breathing heavy, I roll to her side and drag her body over mine like a blanket, not caring about the mess we're making. All that matters is the connection.

I make love to her again, slowly this time, kissing and tasting every inch of her gorgeous body and she falls asleep in my arms. I lie awake wondering what I did right in this life to deserve her and decide I might never know, but I'm not giving her up, not ever.

Audrey wakes hungry and I make us omelets and then change the sheets while she showers. As she dries her hair, I shower and we crawl into bed, entwined like we're both too scared to let go in case it's all a dream.

"Did you really buy Redman Media?"

Audrey's fingers are tracing patterns in the skin on my chest, but she pauses at my question. "Yes. They hurt the people I love. That won't stand."

"I might have overreacted a little. You didn't need to do that."

"I know but it wasn't just me. Linc, Harrison, Beck, and Ryker bought in too."

"They did? Why?"

"Because they hurt Amelia and Xander too, and Ryker."

My fingers skim over her naked shoulder as I consider her words. "They're good friends."

"The best. I don't know what I'd do without them. I'm lucky."

"So are they to have you."

"Oh, I know."

I smile at her confidence which feels renewed. "So you fired everyone? What now?"

"I'm not sure. I'd like to turn the paper into something I can be proud of and maybe merge it with Kennedy."

"People will always love gossip. It's why papers like that sell."

"I know, and I get that, but I hate what they did to Tia. She could've been seriously hurt and there was no consideration for that."

"Maybe it just needs to be run by someone who gives a shit. Have reporters on staff who are respectful."

"Maybe. Or maybe I'll just close it down." Audrey sits up and I get distracted as the sheet slips, revealing her plump pink nipples. "What happened in L.A?"

I tell her all about my suspicions of corruption and how difficult it is for women to get help in situations like that. "Although I've been thinking of giving it up. I want to spend more time with you and Tia now."

"But they need you."

"Lorenzo can handle it."

"But you know the law."

I laugh. "Believe me, Lorenzo knows the law. It's what makes him such a good criminal."

"What if we set up a charity to offer support to these women with confidential advice and guidance and lawyers working pro bono to help free them? We could build on your idea with the app and widen it."

I nod slowly. "I like the idea but the more people involved, the more chances of a corrupt lawyer or member of staff leaking stuff."

"We could start small and maybe play around with it. We certainly have the means, and you could head it up rather than being the lone wolf."

"We could do it together?"

Audrey smiles flirtatiously. "Are you trying to poach me from Kennedy?"

"Never, I know how much your company means to you, but I'd love to have your advice on this."

"I'd love that, too."

Audrey leans in for a kiss and then settles her head against my chest. My eyes drift and I'd happily spend every day here with her.

"Hudson?"

"Hmm?"

"Do you want children?"

My eyes snap open and I roll to look at the woman I love. "Audrey, I want you. If we can have kids, great. If not, then that's great too."

"How would you feel about trying surrogacy and, if that fails, we can look at adoption?"

"I'm happy if you're happy. If we have kids that look just like you and me with your fire and my incredibly good looks then I'll be delighted. If we have children who are nothing like us, who come into our lives by choice later in their lives, then I'll be equally thrilled. And if it only ever ends up being you, me, and Tia then I'll be the happiest man alive, because you're all I need."

The Enemy

Her eyes go wide and glossy. "You really mean that, don't you?"

"All I ever wanted was to be worthy of you, Audrey, and I know I never will be but I don't care. I love every inch of you, and I'm never walking away again."

"Hudson, you've always been worthy of me. You're smart, and kind, loyal, loving, and the kind of man any woman would be lucky to call their own. But they can all go to hell because you're mine and you're stuck with me."

"Nobody I'd rather be stuck with."

I kiss her then and all talk is over for the night. I fall asleep hours later, both of us exhausted, feeling the kind of contentment I never dreamed of.

I'm finally home because she's my home. She always has been.

Epilogue: Audrey

Hudson is gripping my hand so hard, I feel like my fingers might fall off, and it's cute as hell. I glance across at him where Nell, our three-year-old daughter, is cuddled up to his chest. She came to us last year and is the apple of her father's eye. After two years of failed surrogacy, we decided not to put ourselves through anymore and went the adoption route. It hasn't been easy, but Nell is worth every single tear. She's loving and fiery and Hudson says she's just like me. Her parents were killed in a home invasion, and she was put into the system just as we began looking.

It was love at first sight for all of us, including Tia, who adores her baby sister or maybe niece. Either way, it doesn't matter to us. We're a family and that's all that counts in this world, not how it happened or the titles we have.

"You doing okay?"

Hudson shakes his head. "This was a mistake. What if she falls?"

"Hudson, she's been practicing and rehearsing for months. She's got this."

He glares at me as if this is all my fault and I guess in some ways it

220

is. I encouraged Hudson to let Tia spread her wings and fly, and boy did she. Now fifteen, she's doing her first Silk Aerial showcase. She took to it so quickly that it was impossible to hold her back. She's fearless and beautiful and I couldn't be prouder.

"Hey, how's he doing?"

Lincoln and Lottie take the seat beside me with their daughter, Eliza, who is five, and their two-year-old son, John, in honor of my father.

"I think he might puke."

Hudson glares at Lincoln. "I'm not gonna puke. I'm just a little nervous. What if she falls or gets tangled up?"

Lincoln looks up at the stage and winces. "Yeah, I'm with you on this, Hudson. There's no way, Eliza is doing that."

Hudson points at me. "See, even he agrees."

"Will you stop, Tia's got this, and Eliza will do whatever she wants because she has a strong independent woman as a mother."

I turn and wink at Lottie who laughs.

"Momma, look." I follow Nell's pointing finger to see Beck, Xander, and Amelia. Both men are escorting her because for some reason they think her being heavily pregnant means she needs wrapping in cotton wool. I've never seen such protective men and she has to juggle two of them. Ryker and Eden are behind with baby Josh asleep against his father's chest, and their daughter Lydia holding onto her mother's hand. Norrie is behind with Isaac and their other son, Thomas, who is three.

A lot has changed for us these last five years and many more changes are coming but we face all of them head-on because we know we not only have our partners, the loves of our lives, but also each other.

"How is he?" Ryker smirks at Hudson.

"Will people stop asking that? You wait until it's your daughter hanging upside down in mid-air from a piece of silk she'd tangled her legs in."

221

Ryker covers his daughters' ears. "Uh no, not happening."

"I've already laid down the law in our house," Lincoln says cockily.

Hudson rolls his eyes. "Are you stupid?"

Lottie leans across her husband. "No, but he will be celibate if another dumb comment like that comes out of his mouth."

Lincoln looks aghast. "Baby, you know I was only kidding."

Lottie raises her brow. "Yeah, right."

Everyone is talking among themselves, and I lean into my husband as my daughter fingers my hair and sucks her thumb.

"She'll be amazing."

He grins and kisses my cheek. "I know, I can't help but worry though."

"That's one of the reasons I love you."

"Yeah, I thought it was because of my big...."

I give him a warning look and he chuckles. "Get your mind out of the gutter, wife. I was going to say my big yard."

"'Course you were."

The lights dim and we all fall silent as a spotlight hits the stage where three colorful silks hang from a steel beam in the ceiling of the center. Tia walks onto the stage, head high, a wide smile on her face. Dressed in black leggings and a black leotard, she stands beside her silk in the middle. As the music begins, she takes the silk in her hands and performs a perfect straddle mount. Her routine flows from there into *man in the moon*, then into *skirted lady*, and *mermaid* before she performs a perfect *vampire*. She's confident, graceful, and I'm so proud of her I could burst.

Tia performs a perfect roll out and the room erupts with applause and cheers. I turn and see my mom and aunt Heather behind us and she gives me a look, which I can read so easily. She wishes my dad was here, and so do I, but he isn't and life, I've learned, is to be lived every day.

The Enemy

AFTER THE SHOW, WE HEAD BACK TO OUR PLACE, WHICH NOW boasts an extension for our growing family.

"I'll fire up the BBQ."

Harrison heads outside and all the men follow.

"You okay in here or do you need my help?"

Hudson rests his chin on my shoulder as his arms come around my middle. He, Lincoln, Harrison, Ryker, Xander, and Beck have grown close over the years and, despite the rocky start, Hudson and Lincoln are close now. Even running the charity we set up, for abused women to seek shelter, together.

"Go play with the boys, we've got this."

He kisses my neck and I shiver. The passion between us has only grown and, despite waiting for that heat to wane, it hasn't. I want him as much, if not more, now than when we met. The slight grey on the sides of his temple gives him a distinguished look that only makes him hotter.

"I'll make it up to you later."

"Yes, you will."

Heat burns in his eyes as his gaze rakes over me. "Think your mom would have the girls overnight?"

"I'm way ahead of you, handsome. She's taking them home with her when she leaves."

Hudson lifts me against his chest and kisses me deeply, as my arms come around him.

"God, I love you, wife."

"I love you, too, husband."

"No regrets?"

"No regrets."

As he puts me down and heads into our backyard to show the boys his latest obsession, which is fixing up old motorcycles, I know I speak the truth. Our journey to this point wasn't easy but I wouldn't change a moment of it, because now my life is perfect.

~

L Knight

THIS IS THE END OF THE KINGS OF RUIN SERIES, BUT IF YOU'D like to read more from L. Knight then check out Love, Honor, Betray book one in the Tightrope Series.

Books by L. Knight

Kings of Ruin

The Auction

The Consequence

The Unexpected

The Temptation

The Enemy

Tightrope Series

Love, Honor, Betray

Love Lies Bleeding

About the Author

Lia Knight is a romance author of billionaire romance with lots of angst, and heat. Her heroes are super rich, demanding and know exactly what they want, so when they set their sights on the heroines in these books you know the chemistry will explode your kindle. Having written over forty books under a different pen name she wanted to give those rich, bossy heroes fighting for a story a chance have their say and find their HEA.

When she isn't writing, she is binging Yellowstone, The Big Bang Theory, and Bridgerton from her home in Hereford in the UK.

You can contact me at: lknightauthor@gmail.com

Join my Facebook group to get all the latest updates: https://www.facebook.com/groups/KnightsDelights1

Printed in Great Britain
by Amazon

44015035R00138